Frost Heaves

a novel by Alana Terry

"So do not fear, for I am with you; do not be dismayed, for I am your God. I will strengthen you and help you; I will uphold you with my righteous right hand."

Isaiah 41:10

Frost heaves (noun): Upward swelling in soil or roads during freezing conditions, caused by water expanding as it turns to ice.

Note: The views of the characters in this novel do not necessarily reflect the views of the author, nor is their behavior necessarily condoned.

The characters in this book are fictional. Any resemblance to real persons is coincidental. No part of this book may be reproduced in any form (electronic, audio, print, film, etc.) without the author's written consent.

www.alanaterry.com

CHAPTER 1

Jade was being ridiculous. She had no reason to be this nervous. And for what? A testimony? She'd talked about her past plenty of times. Why should doing it on stage in front of her entire church be any different?

Staring at her reflection in the mirror, she wiped her sweaty palms on her pants. *Come on, girl. You've got this.*

The bathroom door swung open, and Jade jumped as her daughter burst through.

"Dezzirae Rose Jackson," Jade snapped, then paused to collect her breath. "You nearly gave me a heart attack."

"I'm sorry, Mama."

"Forget it." Jade let her daughter cling to her leg and adjusted a barrette holding one of Dez's corn rows. "What are you doing here scaring me half to death? Aren't you supposed to be downstairs playing?"

Dez shrugged. "Got bored."

As cute as Dez looked in her *God is my Superhero* T-shirt and sparkling light-up tennis shoes, Jade didn't have

1

time for any extra drama tonight. She gave her daughter a well-rehearsed scowl. "You know you're not supposed to be bugging me right now. I've got to get ready for my talk. How many times do I have to tell you?"

Another shrug.

"Aren't there any other little kids down there?" Jade asked.

Her daughter rolled her eyes dramatically. "Just Mrs. Spencer's grandkids, and they're still babies."

"They're a year younger than you are," Jade huffed.

"Two years." Dez jutted out her lower lip and cocked her head to the side. "And besides, if I stay downstairs, Mrs. Spencer's gonna make me practice my angel lines for the Christmas play, and it's just too hard. Can't I stay up here with you? Mrs. Spencer said it's all right with her."

"Well, it's not all right with me."

"How come?"

"Because I've got to focus on what I'm going to say, and I can't worry about whether or not you're sitting there squirming in your seat." She kissed the top of her daughter's head then pushed her out the door. "Now get yourself back downstairs. And march."

Dez stomped out, staring at her feet. Soon, her light-up tennis shoes distracted her, and she bounced away.

"Oh, that girl," Jade groaned and checked to make sure the backs of her earrings hadn't fallen out. She'd checked them half a dozen times by now, but it was the only thing she could think of to do to get her nerves to settle down.

Lord, you've got to help me get through this.

Her hands were a clammy, sweaty mess, and she washed them again at the sink. After giving herself one more glance in the mirror to make sure everything was right where it was supposed to be, she walked out the door. She had to head downstairs to have a talk with Dez's Sunday school teacher. Mrs. Spencer had agreed to come tonight to watch the kids, and Jade felt it was only right that she give Mrs. Spencer fair warning. Dez had been a handful and a half all day. She was already five but had missed the cutoff for kindergarten by a week and a half. It wasn't even Christmas yet, and already Jade regretted not making a bigger push with the elementary school to accept Dez early. She was acting up nearly every day at the daycare where Jade worked and even gave one of the smaller boys a white-wash when she pushed him down in the snow. Jade had put up with enough of other people's drama in her own life. There was no way she was going to see her daughter turn into a bully.

She was halfway to the stairs when someone called her

name.

Jade turned around. "Hey, girl." She might weigh twice as much as her petite friend, but she didn't worry about squeezing too tight as she wrapped Aisha up in a hug. "I'm heading on downstairs," Jade explained. "Got to talk to Dez's teacher."

"Hold on," Aisha said. "There's someone here to see you."

Jade followed her friend's darting eyes, which landed on a tall white man in a crisp navy blue trooper's uniform. Jade scowled. "Who's that?"

"New trooper," Aisha explained. "He just moved to Glennallen from the bush."

"Is he joining the church or what?" Jade didn't like the way he was staring at her.

The trooper took a few steps closer, and Aisha shuffled nervously. "Sorry, I should have told you sooner," she whispered, but Jade didn't have time to figure out what she was talking about.

The trooper descended on her, hand outstretched enthusiastically. "I'm Ben. You must be Jade."

She gave him a glower. "What makes you think that?"

He gave Aisha a nervous glance, and Jade frowned at him disapprovingly. There were a dozen things annoying about being the only black person in a town as small as Glennallen. Having strangers presume to know her identity was toward the top of the list.

"Aisha pointed you out," he answered.

Oh. That made more sense. Jade cleared her throat and took Ben's hand into her sweaty palm. "Okay. Well, then, what can I do for you, officer?"

"I know you're busy getting ready for tonight's service, but can I talk to you? Won't take more than a minute."

Jade made a point of turning to look at the bear-shaped clock hanging in the church foyer. "Good, because a minute's all I got."

"Is there some place where we could sit down?"

Jade shrugged. "It's a free country, right?" She decided Pastor Reggie wouldn't be needing his office tonight, seeing as how he was on vacation with his family in the Lower 48. She started to head that way then stopped when Aisha touched her arm.

"Sorry," she whispered again. "We started talking outside, and I mentioned that letter. I should have asked you first."

"Yeah, you should have." Jade brushed passed her friend, holding the door open for the trooper. Once they were situated in her pastor's office, she crossed her arms

5

and stared at him. "Like I said earlier, I don't have a lot of time. What's this all about?"

CHAPTER 2

Ben seemed to take a lifetime to decide where and how to sit.

"Are you comfortable?" he asked once they were finally situated.

Jade didn't answer. As far as she saw it, she'd never be comfortable. Not held up by some white cop ten minutes before she was supposed to stand up and share her testimony in front of her whole church.

And for what? That letter was just some stupid ploy. It didn't mean anything. Jade had lived her life in fear. She was an expert on the subject and had eventually learned that fear can't kill you.

And that you don't go to the police when you've got a problem. It was bad enough the daycare where she worked invited the troopers in once a month to read stories to the kids. It was just as well the men who came couldn't read her mind, or they'd never come back.

Jade still had her arms crossed, but Ben didn't seem to

know what to do with his. "I saw the announcement in the newspaper," he finally explained. "Thought I'd come hear you."

Is that all he had to say to her? She stared at Pastor Reggie's stack of *Alaska Fishing* magazines and waited.

He cleared his throat. "I'm new to the area and heard a lot of good things about the church."

"Mm-hmm. I'm sure you did."

Ben glanced at her questioningly. She held his gaze until he looked away.

Finally, she decided it was time to put this conversation out of its misery. "Listen, if Aisha told you about that letter, I want you to know it's all under control. It's totally fine."

"Your friend seemed pretty worried about it."

Jade shrugged. "She gets like that, but trust me. It's nothing. Is there anything else I can do for you?"

Ben leaned forward earnestly, his eyes nearly as large as Pastor Reggie's mounted moose head behind him. "I want you to know this is the kind of thing we take seriously down at the trooper station."

"I bet you do." Jade stood up. "Well, if there's nothing else, officer, I need to get ready."

Ben nodded. "Will you let me know if there's anything I can do to help?"

Help? There was a new one. As far as Jade could tell, policemen like him had *helped* her family far too much already.

She opened the door of the office, mumbling, "I'm sure I'll be all right," as she let herself out.

CHAPTER 3

Before Jade could head downstairs to check on her daughter, Aisha hurried toward her. "Listen, I'm sorry about that trooper. I didn't know he'd want to talk to you right away. I just kind of mentioned it in passing ..."

Jade rolled her eyes, figuring it must be their differences that kept her and Aisha close. Jade had given up any desire for romance or even casual dating, but Aisha would flirt with anybody under the age of fifty. Men in uniform were one of her special weak points. Jade was certain that Ben's trooper's badge was all Aisha had to see to start fawning all over him, and what better way to snag his attention than to blab about some threatening note Jade received in the mail?

"Don't worry about it," Jade mumbled. She couldn't afford to stand here all night and convince Aisha that everything was fine. She'd lost enough time already. Men and women were filing to their seats, smiling at Jade as they passed the family of carved bears welcoming congregants to the service.

On with the show.

She straightened her shirt, smoothed out her pants, and walked into the sanctuary with her head held high, resolving to forget about Aisha and that silly trooper. Jade would bet her paycheck from the daycare that Ben would ask Aisha out before Christmas rolled around. She could have him. Jade had a testimony to focus on.

She made her way to the front row and bowed her head, partly because she wanted to pray and partly so people wouldn't come up and try to strike up any conversations. She clasped her hands in her lap. Were they still shaking? What was it about tonight's testimony that had her so worked up? This was Glennallen. There was hardly anyone she hadn't met in this town, and most of them were already familiar with her story. If anything, tonight was her chance to tell her testimony in her own words so her neighbors wouldn't have to rely on second- and third-hand information.

Nothing like a small town in rural Alaska to get the gossip fires roaring like mad.

Jade shut her eyes. She had to focus her attention on what she was going to say. Had to make sure that her spirit was in the right place.

Help me, God, she prayed when a shrill, whiny voice interrupted.

"Mama!"

Jade snapped her eyes open. "What did I tell you about bugging me when I'm up here?" she hissed, hoping that since she was in the front row, the people behind couldn't detect the annoyance in her expression. If they knew how exasperated she got with her daughter, they might all think twice about inviting her to share tonight.

"I'm so bored down there," Dez groaned and plopped into a chair with a melodramatic sigh.

Jade pinched her arm. "You get yourself back downstairs, or I'm taking away those new light-up shoes, got it?"

Dez turned to her mom once more with wide, pleading eyes. "But I'm old enough to be up here, and I promise to be real quiet."

"Well, you and I both know it's impossible for you to be real quiet. Now get downstairs." The last thing Jade needed was for Dez to hear her testimony tonight and start asking a thousand questions about their past. Jade forced a stern expression as her daughter tilted her head to the side and stuck out her lower lip.

"None of that now." Jade cracked a smile and gave her

daughter a playful swat on the arm. "Go get yourself downstairs or I'll tan your behind."

"No you won't." Dez was smiling now. "You're always saying that, but I don't even know what it means."

"If you don't know what it means, then you should be a lot more worried than you are."

Dez rolled her eyes again, but it was clear to see she was trying hard not to grin.

"Go downstairs, baby," Jade repeated.

"But Mrs. Spencer's gonna make me practice my angel lines."

"Then practice your angel lines, baby. I swear, I've never seen a child more stubborn than you." She let out her breath, softening her voice. As a new Mom, Jade had resolved to never resort to bribery, but that was before she had any idea what it was like to negotiate with a precocious preschooler. "Tell you what. If you're real good, I'll take you out for ice cream after the service."

"But it's too cold," Dez complained. "You can't eat ice cream in the middle of winter."

Jade found herself wondering for a moment if Dez really was her flesh-and-blood child. "Of course you can. Who's been raising you, my little Eskimo baby?" She tickled her daughter's ribs. Dez squealed and ran down the aisle. Jade just hoped she wouldn't trip anyone on her way out of the sanctuary.

With Pastor Reggie out of state, Jade wasn't sure who was going to start the service. These Tuesday night meetings had started out as just a prayer service, but then they added a worship band. Next, Pastor Reggie started to ask people to share their testimonies until finally it was like having a second church meeting in the middle of the week. Jade didn't mind. With the sun setting by 3:30 at the latest during this phase of the Alaskan winter, it wasn't as if there were a whole lot else that she and Dez could be doing. Still, with its being so close to Christmas, she would have thought more people would be out of town traveling, but the sanctuary was as full as it was on a typical Sunday.

Great. On top of the crowd, the couple who usually led worship was out with the flu, and Reggie and his family were out of town, so Jade's talk was going to be the focal point of the evening. It was hard to think that all these people had come just to hear her. Up until recently, Jade hadn't thought of her testimony as anything special, especially when you compared it to the stories of Christians who were saved out of lives of alcoholism or addiction or truly destructive behaviors. She didn't feel ready to talk in front of a group this large, and she certainly didn't feel like she'd had enough time to pray and prepare herself spiritually, but there wasn't anything she could do about it at this point.

One of the elders welcomed everyone to the meeting, offered a quick word of prayer, and then Jade was standing before a church full of people waiting to hear her story.

CHAPTER 4

For all of its rocky start, Jade's testimony picked up until she almost forgot that she was the one speaking. Explaining her history, it felt more like she was one of the dozens of church members sitting in the rows of chairs, listening to her talk about the way God had worked in her life.

She sensed the general interest in the room, and when she talked about the church she grew up in while she was still living in Palmer, Alaska, she saw her audience leaning in as if refusing to miss a single word. She painted them a picture with her words, a picture of the extreme control the leadership at Morning Glory International held over her family, over their congregation. At one point, her eyes landed on Ben, the trooper sitting in the back row, and she saw the same interest and curiosity in his expression as she felt from the rest of the church.

Her hands clammed up for an instant, making it hard to hold onto the microphone. She pried her eyes away from his and avoided looking at that section of the sanctuary for the rest of her speech.

"The funny thing about it," she explained, "is that we would have never used a word like *cult* to describe ourselves. Even though it sounds pretty obvious to other people that what we were involved with was definitely not a healthy Christian church, we didn't know that. We were all taught, not just the kids but our parents too, that it was a grave sin to disrespect our leaders or question their authority in any way. Since we all upheld and respected the Bible, we believed that it would be wrong to go against anything our pastor said. At least once a month the preacher would talk about how Miriam bad-mouthed Moses and was struck with leprosy. The moral was always that we should never question God's leaders. I asked my five-year-old about it a few weeks ago, and that particular part of Scripture hasn't even come up in her Sunday school lessons. She's never even heard of it, but it was more common at our church than Noah's ark or Easter Sunday or any of the other Bible stories.

"It wasn't just Sundays either. We had meetings just about every night of the week, and if you missed something, you needed to have a really good reason or the elders would start to question if you were backslidden. You couldn't miss a service if you were sick, either. You were supposed to come even if you were throwing up a lung and have the elders pray for you and anoint you with oil, right there in front of everybody. And if you didn't recover by the end of the service, that was another time where people would question if you were backslidden. My mom pushed vitamins on all of us like we'd die without them because she knew people would question her spiritual health if her family ever caught a cold."

Jade's hands were still sweaty, but that wasn't because she was staring at the trooper anymore. It was because she knew what part of the story was coming up. She swallowed once, trying to recapture the sense of calm she'd had just a moment earlier.

Unfortunately, she knew that this part of her testimony wouldn't be nearly so easy to get through.

"The biggest problem was that there was no accountability for the elders or the head pastor. If they did something wrong, nobody would dare call them out on it. There was abuse of all kinds. If it's a kind of abuse you can imagine, it was probably happening at Morning Glory, and most of the leaders knew about it. Some of them were honest and God-fearing, but some were the actual perpetrators. Due to this whole idea that you can't question what your leaders do, lots of people got hurt, including children."

She winced, hating to even say the words, hating to remember what she went through.

She was staring at her hands now, wondering if anyone else could see them tremble. She glanced up once and caught Aisha's eye, gleaning an extra dose of strength. If she told her story — even the humiliating and painful parts — maybe she'd help someone else in the future, someone going through the same thing.

"The pastor of Morning Glory took an interest in me, and I got pregnant when I was seventeen. I've since then learned that I wasn't the only underaged girl who found herself in that situation, but the others were encouraged to go have abortions. I refused. I knew what had happened to me was wrong, but the idea of an abortion terrified me. So I told my parents."

She swallowed down the lump in her throat. A few members of the congregation were looking at her with so much sympathy it was like they were trying to squeeze the tears straight out of her body. One woman toward the front was silently weeping.

Jade felt bad for making everyone else depressed. Weren't testimonies supposed to be uplifting? She forced a smile. "Thankfully, my parents believed me and took action. We left the church, which is a whole long and complicated story in and of itself." Jade took in a deep, choppy breath. She wanted to tell them everything. She'd never skipped over this part of her testimony before, but tonight she couldn't get the words out. Couldn't tell them what it really cost her family when they filed charges against the Morning Glory leadership.

She raised her head and glanced at the clock. Mercifully, her time was almost over.

"I won't get into all the details, but the short version is I ended up delivering my healthy daughter, Dezzirae, right before I started my senior year of high school. I later grew to realize that all believers have access to the same God. We don't need a pastor or an elder telling us when we have to go to church or how we should raise our kids or what we should do with our futures. We can all talk to God on our own. And that's not to discount how important it is to have a church family and to have mentors who can give you wisdom and support, even though I'll be the first to admit I still really struggle when it comes to issues of authority after everything we went through."

She glanced once at Ben, who was studying her attentively.

"I'm just really thankful that my parents had the courage to stand up to the leadership like they did because I have other friends whose parents were too afraid to do or say anything." Jade's mouth turned dry, and her words caught somewhere in the back of her throat. A picture of her dad, smiling and serene, flitted uninvited into her mind.

She blinked, forcing herself to stay composed. "I guess that's what I want to end with tonight. A reminder that we're all children of God, whether or not we're a pastor or an elder or have any kind of fancy title, and we all are given the Holy Spirit to lead us and guide us."

She gave the audience a brief nod and turned off the microphone. She wasn't sure if one of the elders was going to close the meeting right away or if they would take a little time for prayer requests before everyone left, but she didn't care.

Walking down the side aisle to keep from distracting anyone, Jade hurried out of the sanctuary. She turned on her car's autostart as she made her way downstairs. If she was lucky, she could grab Dez and have the car warmed up before the congregation was dismissed. The last thing she felt like doing was making chitchat with three dozen people who wanted to talk to her about her life's deepest pain.

Breathless and impatient, she swung open the door of

the church nursery, hoping that Dez might have forgotten the promise of ice cream and instead would settle on some hot chocolate back home.

"How'd it go upstairs?" Mrs. Spencer asked, glancing up from the book she was reading to her twin grandchildren in the rocking chair.

"Fine. Thanks so much for being down here."

"My pleasure."

Jade glanced around the room. "Is Dez ready to go?"

Mrs. Spencer blinked at her. "I'm sorry?"

"I've got the car running," Jade explained as she picked up her daughter's jacket from the nursery coat rack. "Is Dez ready?"

"I thought she went upstairs with you. She told me she was going to ask if that was okay." Mrs. Spencer stood up, setting her girls down on the ground.

"No," Jade answered. "She came up to ask if she could stay, but I sent her back down here." She mentally rehearsed everybody she'd seen in that sanctuary. It was a larger crowd than she'd expected but certainly not big enough that she would have missed seeing her own child.

The dry lump returned to her throat, and her heart started pounding high in her chest.

Where was her daughter?

CHAPTER 5

Jade's voice was hoarse, not from giving her testimony but from shouting into every bathroom stall, storage closet, and hiding place in Glennallen Bible Church. Initially she ignored the terrified feeling in the base of her gut. Dez was just throwing a silent fit somewhere to protest being sent downstairs with old Mrs. Spencer and the "babies." Either that or she was playing an elaborate game of hide-and-seek.

It was what Jade had to believe, and instead of focusing on her fears, she rehearsed all the ways she'd lecture her daughter.

Jade had just finished checking the men's room when Aisha trudged up the stairs, shaking her head. "I checked the nursery rooms and the cleaning closet downstairs. Do you think she went out to the car?"

"I looked there already." Jade glanced around. She didn't want Aisha to see the fear in her eyes. There had to be somewhere they hadn't searched yet. A five-year-old didn't just disappear, especially not on one of the darkest nights of the year. It wasn't even Dez's bedtime, but the sky had been black as midnight for hours already.

Mrs. Spencer hurried toward them. "I just went over everything with Jerry, since he's the go-to guy on maintenance here," she said. "Neither of us could think of any other places in the church that haven't been checked."

Aisha stared at the exit. "People are starting to leave. If we're going to ask for help, we better do it before they're all gone."

At first, Jade had been content searching the church with Aisha and Mrs. Spencer, but if not even the maintenance man could find her daughter, it might be time to recruit more volunteers. She gave a resigned nod, and Aisha scurried to the doorway.

Mrs. Spencer reached out her hand and rubbed Jade's back. "Are you all right, dear?"

Jade nodded. Dez was bright, precocious, and far too intelligent for her own good, with enough common sense to stay indoors when it was negative twenty degrees and pitch-black outside. She also knew how to get on Jade's nerves. "I'm sure she's just hiding out or something." Even as she said the words, she sensed how uncertain they sounded. She tried to force more confidence into her voice. "She does stuff like this all the time."

"I'll go check downstairs again," Mrs. Spencer finally announced. Jade imagined the possible ways she'd punish her daughter once they finally found her. Did Dez have any idea how many people she had worried?

Aisha hurried up with Ben behind her. Of course, she would have turned first to Mr. Trooper. This time, however, Jade couldn't afford to be haughty.

"I hear your daughter's missing?"

Jade forced herself to meet his gaze. "Yeah, I'm sure it's nothing. She likes to be dramatic. But it's so cold outside ..." She let her voice trail off.

"How long has it been since anyone saw her?"

Jade wanted to laugh off his question, but she couldn't. "She came upstairs right before the service started. She wanted to sit with me, and I sent her back downstairs. So the nursery worker thought she was up here, and I assumed she was down there ..." Jade wanted to kick herself. What kind of a mother would take a full hour to realize her daughter was missing? If Dez was outside, she could already be suffering from hypothermia.

Aisha offered her a sympathetic side hug. Ben, however, was far more formal. "You've searched everywhere in the church? You're convinced she's not in here?"

Jade shrugged. "We had three of us looking, and then we got the maintenance man to help. So as far as I know we've checked everywhere."

Aisha kept her arm around Jade's waist, and Jade felt like her tiny friend was the one supporting her. They both looked to Ben, who pulled out a small radio.

"It's cold enough outside and dark enough that I don't want to mess around. I'm gonna call this in." He turned to Aisha. "Why don't you run outside and ask anyone who's able to stay to stick around. We're going to need all the manpower we can get."

Jade couldn't stand the thought of standing by like some helpless damsel. "I'll go with you."

Ben shook his head. "No, you stay. I need you here to pass information on to dispatch. Then you're going to tell me everything you know about that letter."

CHAPTER 6

Jade refused to answer Ben's questions until she could start actively helping with the search. Once she was bundled and outside, Ben began his interview.

"Your friend told me you received a threatening letter. Can you tell me exactly what it said?"

"Yes, I can." Jade hid her hands inside her coat sleeves since she didn't have any gloves. "It said, *Sorry about your dad. You better make sure your little girl's not next.*"

He watched her fidgeting with her sleeves and then handed her his own gloves. She was too tired and cold to refuse them.

"What did the reference to your dad mean? Did you understand that part?"

"Yes," she answered flatly and stared at Ben. He was the real reason why she hadn't shared that part of her testimony at church.

A trooper car pulled into the church parking lot, and Ben excused himself to fill his colleague in. Not a moment too soon. Jade caught Aisha standing under a street lamp and hurried toward her.

"What's going on?" Jade asked.

Aisha's teeth were chattering. "We've looked in all the cars, under all the cars, and around the church. I don't know what else to do but start searching along the road and behind the buildings."

"She wouldn't have come out here. Not without her coat." Jade shook her head. This search was a waste of time. Her daughter had probably found some hiding place in the church, maybe even fallen asleep, and she was going to be grounded until her eighteenth birthday if she didn't show herself soon.

Aisha frowned sympathetically. "Are you doing okay? Do you need anything?"

Jade shrugged. "I need to find out what that girl is doing. I swear, she can be so stubborn."

Ben raced back up. "We've got two men coming out now, and the search and rescue team is standing by in Fairbanks."

"Fairbanks?" Jade wished she could explain what she already knew. Dez wouldn't be out here in this cold.

Ben nodded. "It's a cold, long night. We've got to act fast."

"Well, thank you, Mr. Optimism," Jade muttered under her breath before turning away.

"Wait a minute." Ben reached out his arm, shying away just before touching her elbow. "I still need to know more about that note. You were saying something about your father."

Jade cast her glance over to Aisha, but her friend was already heading off to join the volunteers in the wooded area behind the church.

"What do we need to know about your father?" Ben asked. "What's this letter mean?"

Jade wanted to tell him to mind his own business, but everything regarding her dad was public record anyway. If she told Ben everything now, it'd free up his time to keep looking for her daughter. She took off, following Aisha toward the woods, and Ben hurried to keep up beside her.

"You were listening when I was talking tonight, I assume?" Jade asked, hoping she could save even more time by not having to repeat everything she'd gone through earlier.

"Yeah. I'm so sorry for what happened to you."

Jade didn't have time for sympathy right now. Not from a cop. "My parents went to the police. They pressed charges against the pastor of Morning Star."

29

"Good," Ben inserted forcefully.

His comment derailed her concentration, and it took a second to remember what she was saying. "Well, we did it all. Went to the police, talked with the lawyers. They looked for other witnesses to come forward, but everybody else refused to testify against him."

"They weren't brave enough?"

"No," Jade replied. "They weren't stupid enough. Pastor Mitch had connections all over the Mat-Su valley. The longer the pre-trial period spread out, the more we realized he was going to get away with it. If we got ourselves a miracle, he might get charged with statutory rape, but even that didn't seem too likely. With Pastor Mitch being on a first-name basis with nearly everyone in Palmer, my dad lost hope that he'd ever see the inside of a jail cell."

"That must have been disheartening."

Jade wondered if Ben had taken police training in the art of understatement.

"It was ridiculous," she spat. "And the whole time, we were getting death threats from the people we thought had been our friends, even from some of the parents of girls who went through the exact same thing I did. They treated us like we were turning our backs on God, like we'd lose our salvation if we testified against a monster like that."

Jade gritted her teeth. This wasn't the time to get weepy and weak. This was the time to be angry. Angry, determined, and focused.

"So what happened?" Ben asked the question so softly, Jade wondered if he already knew or maybe suspected the answer.

"My dad attacked him. Confronted him one night when he was coming home and assaulted him with a baseball bat."

She paused to see if Ben had any interjections, if he was going to lecture her about the need to let justice follow its own slow course of action. He remained silent, which wouldn't make telling him the rest of the story any easier.

She was trying to figure out how to continue when someone called out, "Hey, over here!"

Jade raced ahead, panting by the time she made her way through the snow to where the maintenance man was shining the flashlight of his cell phone. "Does this look familiar?" he asked.

Jade's heart was pounding as she stared at the red scarf in the snow. She studied it for a full second before answering, "That's not hers."

"You sure?" Jerry asked, as if Jade might not recognize

her own daughter's scarf.

She nodded, too disappointed to think up any caustic remarks. "And look." She pointed at the lower fringes. "It's been out here a while." She tried to pick it up, but it was frozen to the snow. "See?"

Jerry nodded. "Yeah, I guess you're right. False alarm."

Jade stared around at the towering spruce trees. The snow lay in uneven heaps, without any trace of footsteps. They were wasting their time. "I don't think she's back here."

Jerry shined his flashlight around. "Yeah, I thought she might have left some tracks, but I don't see any."

Jade swallowed hard. "No. No tracks." She had to keep control over her emotions. She had to be strong. It was the only way she was going to find her daughter again.

Lord, show me where she is, she prayed and thought about that letter she'd gotten in last week's mail.

Sorry about your dad. You better make sure your little girl's not next. Would someone from Morning Glory come all the way out to Glennallen from Palmer to hurt her daughter? Was that the way the church was going to get back at Jade for speaking up against their pastor after all these years?

It was far-fetched. It was insane.

But right now, it sounded like the most plausible explanation.

CHAPTER 7

It was nearly eleven before Aisha and Ben forced Jade to warm up indoors. The church had been set up as the search and rescue crew headquarters and was teeming with volunteers and first responders. A helicopter with search lights was circling the area, and the pararescue team from Fairbanks was due to land any minute. Wilderness search and rescue dogs were on their way, and Aisha had already run to Jade's home to get a sample of Dez's dirty laundry so the canines could try to pick up her scent.

Jade couldn't believe any of this was happening.

"If your daughter wandered off, we're going to find her." Ben pulled a pen out from his breast pocket. "But until then, we need to examine every possible option. I want you to think of anyone who may have wanted to hurt you or your daughter. We need to make a list of possible suspects."

Jade's hands were so cold even after wearing Ben's gloves she could hardly hold onto her mug of coffee. She blinked at him.

Aisha gave Jade what must have been her fiftieth hug of the night and stood up. "I'm going to see if I can call in a few more volunteers. Be back soon." Jade watched her friend depart, feeling a wistful longing for something she was too tired and confused to name.

"Suspects," Ben repeated. "Who might have sent you that letter, for one thing?"

That one wasn't hard to answer. "Anybody back at Morning Glory."

"No good. It's too broad."

"Well, what do you want?" Who did this cop think he was, making Jade feel like a criminal being brought in for questioning?

"I need names. Specific names. And details. Where they live. Who had the most motive to hurt you or your family."

"I don't know." Jade didn't try to hide her exasperation. She focused on a small speck of dirt beneath her fingernail, begging herself to stay composed. Once she got her daughter back safely, she'd allow her tears to fall. Until then, she had to seize control of her emotions.

Ben sighed and softened his expression. "Look, I know how hard this is for you."

Jade didn't believe him, but she had no energy left to argue.

"Let's back up a little bit, okay? Can I assume the note you received was from someone at your old church?"

She sniffed and nodded. "Yes." Who else had that much reason to hate her as well as her father enough to send a letter like that?

Ben nodded. "I'd have to agree."

She tried not to let him see her roll her eyes. Did he think that listening to her testimony once and spending some time together outside in the cold made him an expert on her and her family situation all of a sudden?

"Do you think it could be the pastor retaliating?"

Jade scoffed. "I seriously doubt that."

"We can't take anything for granted," Ben reminded her, as if she wasn't already keenly aware of the gravity of her situation. He frowned. "I hate to be indelicate here, but putting together what you said in church this evening, would I be right to assume that this pastor, this …"

"Pastor Mitch." Jade supplied the word for him.

"Pastor Mitch," Ben repeated. "Am I right to assume that he is your daughter's biological father?"

Jade kept her eyes on his shoulder. "That's correct." Next thing he'd do was find two dolls and tell her to show him how it happened.

Ben sighed. "Well, if you ask me, that makes him a pretty significant suspect right there. Your father attacked him, you exposed him for what he was, and your daughter is his biological offspring."

Jade stared at him. Had he come up with that all by himself?

He looked at her, waiting.

"Problem with that line of reasoning is that he's dead." Jade's voice was flat.

"He is?"

"Yeah. As of last fall." Jade had read the obituary herself, two paragraphs posted online. *Pastor Mitch Cobb, beloved church leader, husband, and friend is now rejoicing eternally in the kingdom of heaven ...*

The irony wasn't lost on Jade to see the pastor who'd preached nothing but faith healings succumb to cancer. She stood up.

"I'm going to see if Aisha needs help making those phone calls." She took a step away, but Ben grabbed her by the hand.

She yanked herself free instinctively and hissed, "Don't touch me."

"I'm sorry. I know this is difficult for you."

"Actually, officer, I don't think you do." She refused to meet his eyes, knowing that if he was staring at her with even a fraction of the compassion she could detect in his voice, she'd break down and never make it through this night.

"I really want to ask you a few more questions. Do you need a break first?"

The last thing she wanted to do was to sit here with her daughter missing and talk with this trooper, but she was too tired to argue. She shook her head. "No, I'm okay."

"You're sure?"

"Yeah." The sooner they got this meeting over with, the sooner she could go back and join the citizens of Glennallen who right now were braving the ever-dropping temperatures to look for her daughter. It was only a few questions. What was she so afraid of?

She took in a deep, choppy breath and gave him a nod. "I'm ready. Let's do this."

CHAPTER 8

Once she started, it was easy for Jade to come up with name after name of members of Morning Glory International who might want to hurt her family. There was Elder Keith, formerly one of her dad's best friends and the one who'd been the most vocal about trying to cover up the abuse. He even offered to pay the family five thousand dollars if Jade told everyone that the child she carried belonged to some boyfriend from school.

After the allegations were exposed to the public, various individuals delighted in telling Jade and her family how sinful they were to bring such outlandish charges against their pastor. Even though a DNA test could easily reveal the child's parentage, most members of the church preferred to think that Jade and her family made the entire thing up. Halfway into her pregnancy, the pastor's wife, Lady Sapphire, forced Jade into a bathroom stall and yanked up her blouse because the baby bump looked like nothing more than a little extra weight on an already heavyset teenager. It wasn't until Lady Sapphire felt Pastor Mitch's child kicking in Jade's womb that she even recognized the pregnancy was anything more than a lie and a ruse meant to tear down Morning Glory International and its ministry across the Mat-Su valley.

Ben's suspect list had grown to ten different names by the time Aisha sat down beside them. "We've got a few more volunteers on their way to relieve the ones who've been out the longest."

Jade couldn't believe she was hearing this. Couldn't believe there was actually a search team at this moment scouring the woods surrounding the church to look for her five-year-old daughter. As hard as it was to picture Dez wandering off into the cold without a coat or flashlight, the idea of an abduction was even more unfathomable.

If Dez had been taken, whoever had her was twisted. Demented. Who would want to harm a child? The thought made Jade even more terrified. Would the night ever end?

"I need more coffee," she told Aisha, who looked about as tired as Jade felt. But she wasn't going to sleep until her daughter was found. She finally understood what was going through her dad's mind when he found out what Pastor Mitch had done to her. Why he'd grabbed that baseball bat and waited to ambush his prey. It made sense now, that rage. That protective instinct. No parent could sit back and watch someone destroy their child's life, not without taking matters into their own hands.

Jade thought back to the vows people made back in the time of the Old Testament. *May the Lord deal with me, be it ever so severely* ... Right now, there didn't seem to exist human language that could describe what Jade would do to anyone who even threatened Dez's safety.

May God have mercy on their soul, she thought. But even God's mercy was too good for anyone who hurt her daughter.

CHAPTER 9

When midnight came, the temperature had dropped to thirty-two below, and there were now both helicopters and rescue dogs involved in the search. Nobody said so, but Jade knew everyone was thinking the same thing.

A five-year-old in this cold could never survive until morning. A soft blanket of snow fell, diffusing the search lights so it looked like Jade was looking at the world through an eerie haze.

Where was Dez?

Aisha was still outside, but most of the original volunteers had gone home, replaced by others ready to search through the night if necessary. Jade watched the snow falling with a forlorn resignation, knowing that in another hour or less, any tracks that might have led the rescue teams to her daughter would vanish forever. Then again, maybe the snow was actually a blessing. Maybe it would provide Dez with a blanket to keep her warm through the night.

No, she wouldn't think like that. Dez wasn't out in this cruel winter climate. And she hadn't been kidnapped or harmed by anyone from Morning Glory, either. She was still inside the church, warm and safe and sleeping peacefully. Jade would be so relieved to find her daughter perfectly unharmed that she wouldn't even dole out all the punishments she'd been daydreaming about earlier.

Was it really possible that this was the same night she'd stood in front of her church and shared her testimony? Just a few hours ago, being abused, pregnant, and shunned by everybody but her parents was the most traumatic experience Jade could imagine, the most challenging trial she'd ever have to endure.

Until now.

Dez was born out of despair, hurt, and humiliation, but Jade had loved her from the beginning. Throughout the pregnancy, even with those chaotic hormones and that relentless confusion, Jade had been protective of her baby. Her love for her child was no small miracle considering Jade had never been overly fond of children. She wasn't like other girls who dreamed of nothing but marriage and motherhood. Jade had goals too, but hers involved feats like winning the Nobel Peace Prize, working relentlessly to help the nation achieve racial equality, and earning her law degree before her twenty-fifth birthday.

At first, she convinced herself that her teenage pregnancy did nothing but put those plans on hold. The older Dez got, the more Jade had come to accept that her prior ambitions would have to go unrealized. As a single mother working for minimum wage at a daycare, Jade was lucky if she managed to pay her heating bill every winter. How was she supposed to put aside money for education, let alone find the time to take any classes?

Some days, Jade was depressed at the way life had derailed all her prior dreams, but now she hated herself for ever wanting anything more than to have her daughter by her side, safe and sound.

She longed for a kind word from her mother, a friendly hug from her father, but they were both gone. Her father met his end shortly after attacking Pastor Mitch with that baseball bat, and Mom's high blood pressure and failing heart couldn't hold up to the stress the family endured in the aftermath of the assault.

It wasn't fair. Because of Pastor Mitch, Jade had lost both of her parents.

"Here you are. I thought maybe you'd gone back inside the church to warm up."

Jade turned to see Mrs. Spencer, Dez's Sunday school

teacher, and said, "I thought you went home hours ago."

"I did but just long enough to drop the twins off with their mom and grab warmer clothes." She looked down at her snow boots. "I'm so sorry about what happened. I was sure she was upstairs with you."

Jade didn't want to be angry with Mrs. Spencer. She wanted to accept her apology. But how different would this evening have looked if the old woman had just followed Dez upstairs instead of sending a five-year-old up to the sanctuary by herself? In a town as small and safe as Glennallen, with a church where everybody knew everybody else, Dez should have been fine. But the night was so dark, and the temperatures were still dropping.

Jade ignored Mrs. Spencer's apology, prayed that God would forgive her for her bitterness, and continued tramping through the snow in search of her daughter.

CHAPTER 10

"Ben's at the church looking for you. He said he found a warmer coat and some snow boots you can borrow."

Jade could barely process Aisha's words. "What time is it?" she asked.

"Almost two. I know you don't want to stop, but you need to come in and at least warm up."

Jade surprised herself by not protesting when her friend put her arm around her and started leading her in the direction of the church. Her legs ached, and everything below her knees was numb from cold and wet from the deep heaves of snow.

Aisha didn't try to talk while they walked, and Jade was grateful. She was too tired and emotionally drained to carry on any sort of conversation. It was good of Aisha to still be here. Most of the other volunteers had returned to their heated homes, leaving the search to the rescue dogs and professionals. If Dez had wandered outside, she would have been found by now, or at least someone would have stumbled over her tracks.

Which only left one conclusion.

The air inside the church was so hot compared to outside that Jade could hardly breathe. She had to find some way to escape from the feeling of intense heaviness that threatened to crush her under its impossible weight. She turned to head back out.

Ben hurried toward her. "Wait a minute. You need to warm up."

Jade braced herself against the sternness in his voice. "I need to find my daughter." The urge was primal, unshakeable. She couldn't reason it away or depend on common sense at the moment. She had to get Dez back, and she wasn't going to rest until her daughter was safe.

"We've checked on a few of the leads," Ben told her, holding up his list of suspects. "Don't worry, we'll find her."

Jade knew he was in no position to make any promises, but she clung to his words nonetheless.

He pointed toward the stairs. "One of the ladies from church brought you heavier clothes. And they've got basins of hot water in the kitchen for warming up your feet. Why don't you head down there now, and I'll be with you in a few minutes. I have some more questions for you about your old church."

Jade tried to read between the lines. If Ben was focusing all his attention on Morning Glory, did that mean he was convinced this was a case of kidnapping or intentional foul play?

It was a possibility Jade wasn't willing to accept. Not yet. Dez was a tiny little wisp, feisty as anything, but small enough she could roll herself into the size of a beach ball. Couple that with her stubbornness and her ability to fall asleep anywhere, and she might be perfectly safe in a cupboard or a drawer in this nice, heated church, somewhere nobody'd thought to look yet.

"Where are you going?" Ben called as Jade headed to the Sunday school rooms.

"I want to check everything one more time," she answered, thankful he didn't protest.

Dez was here. Jade knew it. Because if her daughter was outside in the cold or if she'd been abducted and was in danger, Jade would know. Her heart would cleave in two, making it impossible to think, to speak, to function. The fact that Jade was still standing on her own two legs was all the proof she needed that her daughter was alive and safe.

All she had to do now was find her.

CHAPTER 11

"I thought you were going to change into dry clothes," Ben said when he found Jade rummaging through the Christmas pageant costumes in the storage closet downstairs.

"I will. Soon." In a pile of shepherds' garb, Jade spotted a splash of color that might have been one of her daughter's barrettes. Tossing costumes haphazardly aside, she reached down to find it was only a fake jewel from a wiseman's crown.

Ben's voice was both firm and gentle. "You need to change your clothes and get warmed up. Then we can look around the church more."

"She is really good at hide-and-seek." Jade spoke the words as if she were trying to convince Ben of what they both knew was a lie. She couldn't stop herself. "At the daycare, she's always going around hiding in cabinets and drawers. Once she even crawled into the toy chest and fell asleep beneath all the dress-up clothes. She's here. I know

49

that she's got to be here."

Ben touched her gently on the shoulder. "I've already searched this whole closet myself. Twice."

Something about Ben's touch shook her to her core. Or maybe it was the way her feet had finally started to thaw and were now screaming with pain. Her whole body began to tremble.

"She's got to be here," she repeated, her voice weak and almost as shaky as her core.

Ben rubbed her gently on the shoulder, and she turned to him as tears streamed hot down her face. "Do you promise that you're going to do everything you can to get my daughter back to me?" The inherent confession in her question, the admission that she knew her daughter was in danger, brought on another round of trembling and a sob that nearly worked its way out of her clenched throat.

Ben reached out and touched her chin, tilting her face up until she was staring straight at him. Wiping a tear away gently with his calloused thumb, he nodded. "I promise. Now let's go get you warmed up."

CHAPTER 12

While her feet soaked in a pan full of hot water, Jade sipped at some tea. Her legs ached as they continued to thaw. She would have preferred to be out in the cold, at least able to convince herself she was doing something useful.

Aisha sat with her and prayed, and Mrs. Spencer joined in for a little while too. Jade was thankful for their concern but couldn't help wondering if all that time and energy they put into their prayers would be better spent hunting for her daughter.

"Brought you something to eat." Ben stepped up and handed her a ham and cheese sandwich on a paper plate. Jade hated sandwiches and had since elementary school. Besides, how could she eat now when she didn't know if her daughter was kidnapped or lost in the woods or maybe already dead?

"You should have it," Aisha urged, and Jade nibbled at the whole grain crust with disinterest. Aisha stood up to get more tea.

"I've been going over the notes from the pre-trial," Ben said, crushing any hope Jade had that she might be able to stomach her food. He sat down across from her with a frown. "I read about your father."

Jade shrugged. She should have figured he'd find out the truth sooner or later.

Ben sighed. "I know it doesn't change what happened, but for what it's worth, I'm sorry."

She glared at him. "Why? It wasn't your fault." What right did he think he had, probing into her past and making her relive that awful pre-trial period? Did he seriously think that now was an appropriate time to bring it up?

Ben shuffled some pages he was carrying. "Well, we've managed to narrow down the suspect list."

She wished she could turn her ears off. She wasn't ready to face the reality that this missing child case was morphing into an abduction investigation. It was too much for her to handle. She buried her head in her hands.

"I'm so sorry you're going through this." He sounded sincere, but how could he understand even a fraction of what she was experiencing?

She met his gaze. "Do you have children, officer?"

He shook his head.

"I didn't think so," Jade mumbled. And yet here he was pretending to be sympathetic. What would he know about parenthood or the terror that comes from realizing you failed to protect your own child?

She didn't need more tea. She didn't need a stupid sandwich. She needed her daughter. How many times had she lost her temper or gotten angry at Dez, who was every bit as sassy as Jade had been at that age? She'd take it all back now if she could, the drawn-out lectures, the angry shouts, that infamous Mom stare she'd perfected when Dez was still in her terrible twos.

"It must be hard working with the police after what happened to your dad." Ben's voice was soft, so quiet Jade wondered if she should simply pretend not to have heard.

He didn't know anything. He couldn't.

Jade hated him. She hated his condescending pity, his flashy blue uniform and everything it represented in her past. She hated the fact that she was sitting here like a helpless victim instead of marching outside and leading the investigation to find her daughter.

Aisha returned, passing Jade a new cup of tea and taking her empty mug from her. "Maybe you should get some rest." Aisha had been Jade's best friends for years, but tonight was a clear and obvious reminder of their differences. If Aisha were a mother herself, she'd understand how insulting the suggestion was. Sleep? How could she expect Jade to sleep on a night like this?

"I think that's a good idea," Ben replied, as if his opinion settled the matter. "I can drop you off at your place if you want."

Jade crossed her arms. "I'm not going anywhere."

"I promise I'll call you with any updates."

She shook her head. "I'm staying here."

"Maybe you could rest on one of the couches," Aisha suggested softly. Jade rolled her eyes. Maybe Aisha was the kind of girl who could fall asleep on a whim, even with the investigation of her daughter's kidnapping ongoing in the next room, but Jade wasn't.

"I'm fine. I just need to get more coffee." She stood up.

"Are you sure?" Aisha asked with a pained expression on her face.

"Positive," Jade grumbled. She brushed past her friend and stormed over to the coffee pot, unable at the moment to look at her compassionate eyes without breaking.

She'd need all the energy she could get to make it through the night.

CHAPTER 13

"Jade? Excuse me. Are you awake?"

She jumped at the sound of the familiar voice, banging her head on some kind of shelf. "What in the ..."

"Shh." His tone was calming. Soothing. "It's all right. It's me, Ben. I just had a few questions for you."

She blinked. Why wasn't she in bed? How could she have fallen asleep?

"You're in the church closet." Ben reached down and picked up a wise man costume Jade had been holding.

Her brain wrenched in protest as every single horrible replay of last night crashed around her memory banks. "Did you find my daughter?" She stood again, this time knocking over a box of flannelgraph Bible characters before stepping out of the closet.

Glancing down the church hallway, she studied those around her, trying to figure out if Ben woke her up with good news or bad. Nearly all the faces were unfamiliar: police officers from Anchorage, troopers from the surrounding areas, search and rescue teams deployed from God alone knew where. They all looked tired and worried, not a good sign, but at least they looked busy, which meant the investigation was still ongoing.

Which meant there was still hope. Right?

She braced herself for whatever news Ben had for her.

"Do you need more coffee?" he asked. "A sandwich?"

She shook her head. Why couldn't he just get straight to the point?

"Let's take a seat."

As they passed through the church kitchen, she glanced at the time. Just after five in the morning, with at least another five hours to go before the sun even thought of rising. How much snow had fallen last night? How long could a child as small as Dez survive this long outside?

Jade clenched her fists and jutted up her chin. Whatever news Ben brought her, she was ready. Anything was better than this uncertainty, this waiting.

"What can you tell me about Keith Richardson?" he asked.

"Elder Keith?" It had been years since she stepped foot in Morning Glory's ornate church building, but the title came to her out of habit.

Ben nodded.

"He was one of my dad's best friends." Jade wondered what kind of information Ben was looking for. What did he want her to say?

"He's the leader of Morning Glory now." From Ben's tone, Jade couldn't tell if he was asking her a question or stating a fact.

"Yeah, he took over after Pastor Mitch died."

"The church website still calls him Elder Keith, not pastor."

Jade shrugged. It was no surprise. The church would remain loyal to Pastor Mitch no matter how horrific his crimes had been in life.

"Was Keith Richardson upset when your family went to the police about your pastor?"

She nodded. At first, she was thankful to Ben for his discretion. Thankful he didn't use words like *rape* or *abuse*, labels that had been thrust on Jade's shoulders since she was a teenager. But the more she thought of it, the more his question smacked of condescension. Did he think she couldn't handle hearing the truth spoken out loud? Did he think she was that fragile? She sat, waiting for what he would say next.

"Have you been in contact with Keith Richardson since you left Morning Glory?" The question was direct. Abrupt.

As if for a moment he'd forgotten that Jade was the victim's mother and not a suspect herself.

"We stopped having anything to do with him," she answered. "He was one of the most vocal opponents of us going to the police. He even offered to pay my family money to keep it quiet."

"But you haven't had any contact with him recently?" Ben was staring at her with an intensity that made her heart race. What was he suggesting?

She shook her head. "No. Why?"

Ben pulled out her cell phone. It was the first time Jade had realized it wasn't in her pocket like normal. "Where'd you get that?"

He didn't answer her question but just said, "Keith Richardson left you five different text messages in the past half hour."

Jade yanked the phone out of his hands. "What did he say?" Elder Keith had been like an uncle to her when she was younger. His daughter Trish had been her best friend, and they'd promised to go to college together and be roommates and study pre-law together. Jade knew for a fact Trish had been one of the girls Pastor Mitch abused, but even if Elder Keith was aware of the crime, he was too loyal to Morning Glory to ever try to put a stop to it.

And now he was messaging her after Dez disappeared?

She scrolled through the texts, trying to will her hand steady.

It's Elder Keith. Are you there?

We need to talk. Can I call?

I know it's early, but this is important.

Are you getting any of my messages?

Jade's stomach flopped, and she physically recoiled from her phone when she read his last message.

I know what happened to your daughter.

CHAPTER 14

Aisha and Mrs. Spencer had both gone home, so it was Ben who was left to do what he could to soothe Jade's nerves.

"It's going to be all right," he assured her. "We've got someone in Palmer on their way to speak with Richardson right now. They're going to contact us as soon as they find anything out."

Ben sat patting her hand. It was a silly, fruitless gesture, but she couldn't find the words to ask him to stop.

"I'm so sorry you're going through this."

She'd lost track of how many times he'd said this or something similar. If he was so sorry, why wasn't he doing more to get her daughter back? She gritted her teeth, hating how out of control she felt.

"I went through something a little similar. I know it's not the same thing as missing a child." Whatever Ben was going to say next, Jade was certain it wouldn't be helpful, but he went on, and she stared at the wall blankly, too numb to speak.

"My dad was a cop down in LA during the race riots. He wasn't on duty that night, but he got called in anyway. My mom had taken me and my sister to my grandma's house in Redondo Beach to get away from the heat, and she kept us up late to pray for dad's safety. He didn't come home that morning, and by the next night we still hadn't heard anything. It wasn't until the following day his partner found out where my mom was to tell her that my dad had been killed."

Jade didn't speak.

"I know it's different when it's your parent and not your child, but I remember that day of waiting, how hard it was. If you were to look at my mom, you might have thought she aged a decade in twenty-four hours. I'm sorry for what you're going through."

Jade tried to swallow, but the lump in her throat made it impossible.

"I guess that's something we do have in common though," Ben said quietly. "Both of us losing our dads."

She didn't want to agree. Didn't want to acknowledge that what this trooper went through was anything like what she'd endured the night her dad died. Her father had known the police were coming for him. He had no regrets about what he did to Pastor Mitch. When it seemed clear that his daughter's abuser would go free, he'd taken justice into his own hands, and he was prepared for his arrest. He was ready. He'd even called some of his family members, people outside Morning Glory who were still speaking to him, and made some arrangements to make it easier for Jade and her mom while he was in jail.

What he wasn't prepared for was six white men barging into his home in the middle of dinner and making the entire family lie face down on the floor. Jade was eight months pregnant at the time, and when one of the officers shoved her roughly, her dad intervened.

The cop shot.

Her father was dead before he even hit the ground.

And now Jade was sitting here across from this white trooper whose white father had also been a cop. A white cop. The kind Jade had learned to fear. Had learned to hate.

And yet he'd been a victim of senseless violence as well. A victim of the racist disease that had plagued their country for centuries.

She felt sorry for Ben and what he and his family must have gone through. But she still wasn't sure she wanted his sympathy. Still wasn't sure he'd earned the right to presume that he could understand her situation.

She hung her head, listening to the drone of the church fridge and the muttered voices of those around her, trying to imagine what it would be like to live in a world where fathers always came home when they promised they would, where police — *all* police — could be trusted to protect the vulnerable.

Where five-year-old girls didn't disappear without a trace, leaving nothing behind but nameless fears and unbearable uncertainty.

CHAPTER 15

If Ben wanted help writing Keith Richardson's life story, he should have asked someone who'd actually managed to sleep last night. Jade filled in the details she could remember, but half an hour later, the sketch was still far from complete. She didn't even remember what Elder Keith had done for a living.

After Ben checked to make sure her phone was still set to record incoming and outgoing calls, Jade tried calling the number Elder Keith used to text her, but it went immediately to a generic message stating that his voice mailbox was full. She texted him back. Once. Twice. What did he know about Dez?

Then came more of Ben's questions. "Was Keith Richardson ever violent?"

Jade shook her head. "No. He was Pastor Mitch's right-hand guy, a yes man. He never wanted to rock the boat or do anything besides what Pastor Mitch specifically told him." Jade hated the way that even after she'd freed herself from Morning Glory's authoritative presence in her life she still referred to its leaders by their titles. It was as if she were still a little twelve-year-old girl being told that to disrespect her pastor, even in the privacy of her own thoughts, would be as sinful as spitting in the face of Jesus himself.

"You said Keith was angry with your dad about exposing the abuse."

Jade nodded. "Yeah. They got into quite a few fights. Just yelling though."

"Never violent?" Ben pressed.

"No. Not that I ever saw." In truth, it was her father who had the temper, her father who would raise his voice. Her father who had attacked Pastor Mitch with a baseball bat. Who had died trying to protect his daughter from being manhandled by a white cop.

What did Ben think? Did he side with the Palmer police captain? Just two days after her father's murder prompted an internal investigation, the cop who shot him was reinstated. As far as Jade knew, he was still serving on the police force. The policeman went on record claiming he'd been afraid for his life, and nobody thought to second-guess him. Nobody questioned why six armed men were entitled to use deadly force on a father trying to shield his child.

The unspoken consensus was that her father deserved to die, shot point-blank in front of his wife and the pregnant daughter he was trying to defend.

"What can you tell me about Elder Keith's family?" Ben asked.

Jade was grateful for the chance to distract herself from memories of her father's murder. "He had a daughter in the same grade as me and a son who was already grown and out of the house."

"What about his wife?"

Jade shrugged. "She was the church receptionist. Pretty quiet and mousey." Just like all the women at Morning Glory were taught to be. "Mrs. Richardson was good friends with Pastor Mitch's wife. In fact, I think they were related, cousins or something like that." Jade hardly ever thought about her pastor's wife, but now a picture of Lady Sapphire popped into her head uninvited, the cold hardness in her eyes, the feel of her sharp fingernails pinching her skin. The sound of her hiss as she accosted Jade in the bathroom and whispered, "If you bring charges against my husband, I fear for your soul in the afterlife."

Jade could still remember the hint of wintergreen on Lady Sapphire's breath before she plastered on her fake smile and stepped out the bathroom like a queen presiding over her subjects. Which, in terms of the Morning Glory hierarchy, was exactly what she was. Pastor Mitch was the ruling dictator, and Lady Sapphire was his beloved confidante, the hauntingly beautiful reigning figurehead, whose words of exhortation were elevated to as high a level as her husband's.

Lady Sapphire was known for her vivid dreams, which all members of Morning Glory were taught to uphold as infallible as the Scriptures themselves. The story of Lady Sapphire's dream the night before she married Pastor Mitch took on the role of both legend and prophesy, the promise of a child who could carry on Pastor Mitch's apostolic ministry in the state of Alaska. Years later the medical community pronounced Lady Sapphire infertile, but she persisted in believing in that miracle offspring, the fulfillment of God's promise given decades earlier.

But Ben wasn't asking Jade about the pastor's wife. He was asking about Elder Keith, and Jade took pains to answer each question methodically even though her brain was screaming from exhaustion. Elder Keith was, for the moment, the force's primary person of interest. Jade didn't understand why he would have bothered texting her if he was the guilty one, but Ben explained that the best possible outcome would be if Elder Keith claimed responsibility and made a demand for ransom.

If Elder Keith wanted money in exchange for Dez's return, he had incentive to keep her safe.

The teams were continuing to search outside, waiting for daybreak when a new round of local volunteers could be called in. Jade was grateful the troopers and police and everyone else involved in the search and rescue were being so thorough, but the more she thought about her past at Morning Glory, the more she had to admit that Dez's disappearance was almost certainly an abduction.

It made sense. The warning letter, the texts from Elder Keith.

Jade wondered when she'd hear back from the police sent to question him in Palmer.

She didn't think she had the energy to withstand even another five minutes of this torturous waiting.

CHAPTER 16

A little later in the morning, Mrs. Spencer showed up with four cartons of eggs and other supplies donated from Puck's Grocery store. Aisha came in just a few minutes later. While Mrs. Spencer set about making breakfast for the rescue workers, Aisha took Jade into Pastor Reggie's office to pray.

Over half a decade after leaving Pastor Mitch's church, it was still difficult for Jade to remember that she didn't need a pastor's permission or an elder's blessing to lift her requests up to God. She'd been trained so thoroughly by the Morning Glory leadership to rely on church hierarchy to grab heaven's attention that it took her years to learn to pray on her own. Even now, with the stress and anxiety so heavy on her, she found it nearly impossible. Having Aisha with her helped a little. Aisha was a newer Christian, having come from a Muslim background before she got saved and moved to Glennallen, but Aisha seemed to excel at the gift of prayer. As she raised her requests to God, Jade felt a fraction of the weight she'd been carrying lift from her shoulders. As soon as they said *amen*, the burden returned, but at least the short reprieve convinced her that God was listening.

He had to be. There was no one else now to watch out for her daughter. No one else to guarantee her protection. What was Dez thinking right at this moment? What fears or tortures was she enduring? It was too horrific to fathom. Jade had done everything in her power to shield Dez from the details of her past. Whenever her daughter asked who her daddy was, Jade told her that God was her Father and for now that's all she needed to know. The thought that the same people who had witnessed Jade's most humiliating abuse had now kidnapped her daughter was inconceivable.

Ben was still holding onto hope that Elder Keith was trying to contact her with a ransom demand, but Jade knew Morning Glory better than that. The church and its leadership had all the money they wanted thanks to a guilt-inducing tithing system. To remain in good standing, church members had to pledge up to thirty percent of their annual income and even provide tax statements to verify their faithfulness. It was more likely Dez's kidnapping was about power, the real currency Morning Glory's leaders cared about.

To continue to wield their power, Morning Glory enacted policies that could have been taken straight out of a dictator's rulebook. If a church member questioned the pastor, if they fell short in their financial giving, if rumors circulated regarding some petty offense, they were paraded in front of the congregation for public shaming. Once a young nurse was excommunicated simply because Lady Sapphire had a dream accusing her of a spirit of lust. When anybody was forced out of the congregation like this, their history was completely purged from the church records. Even their tithe statements — public record from Morning Glory's earliest days — were altered, their contributions listed anonymously. Jade was sure her own family had been erased as well, probably even more zealously given the way they had exposed Morning Glory's ugliest secrets to the world.

How many times had she been told to respect her leaders, not to question their authority? What she and her family had done was unforgivable. She wasn't sure what kind of changes had taken place after Pastor Mitch's recent death from cancer, but if things were anything like what they were before, it wasn't difficult to imagine the church finding a way to get back at her.

But why now? If Morning Glory was so angry with

Jade and her family, if they were bent on retribution, why did they wait five years after Jade's pregnancy to act? What had changed? Was it because Jade had shared her testimony in public? Last night's audience couldn't have been larger than forty. Besides, her testimony was far more about God's grace delivering her from a life of church dictatorship and legalism than it was about besmearing Morning Glory's reputation.

It didn't make sense.

And how was Elder Keith involved? Even though he hadn't wanted Jade's family to get the police involved, he'd always been soft-spoken, docile, and in most cases completely unintimidating. Had his rise to leadership after Pastor Mitch's death corrupted him?

Jade hated to confront these questions alone. She longed for a word of wisdom or encouragement from her parents more than ever. It wasn't fair that God took both of them away. They never saw their granddaughter crawl or walk or eat solid foods or babble her first words. Why had God added sorrow upon sorrow in Jade's life like that?

In the book of John, Jesus promised his disciples not to leave them as orphans, but that's exactly what happened to Jade. She was an orphan, a single mom doing her best to provide for her daughter, working a menial job because it was the only thing she could find that would allow her to stay (mostly) on top of the bills and keep her daughter nearby. She'd tried so hard, working herself ragged, agonizing over every one of Dez's cuts and scrapes and ear infections and cold viruses. How many times had she begged God to give her strength to handle life as a single mother?

And now Dez was gone. Had God forsaken her? Was such a thing possible?

She thought of Jesus' words on the cross. If the Son of God could feel abandoned by his heavenly Father, why couldn't she? All Bible promises aside, Jade had never felt more betrayed. Here she was doing everything she could think of to live a godly Christian life. She brought her daughter to Sunday school, to Glennallen Bible's midweek services. They read stories from Scripture together each night before bed. Each night, that is, until last.

And if Jade felt so abandoned, how must Dez feel right this instant?

Mrs. Spencer handed Jade a paper plate with scrambled eggs, bacon, and toast. Jade had no appetite but picked at the food methodically, hoping it would get her mind off her troubles.

By the time she finished breakfast, she was still just as

tormented as she'd been before, but now she had a stomachache on top of all her other worries.

CHAPTER 17

"I want to thank everyone for your continued support in this search and rescue," Ben told those gathered in the church kitchen. The smell of bacon grease made Jade queasy while people around her ate their hearty breakfasts.

The sun still hadn't come up yet, and when it did, they'd have less than five hours of functional daylight to keep searching for Dez outside. Jade wondered how long it would take until the teams gave up. How long was a child that little expected to survive in this cold? At least this morning the sky was overcast, giving Glennallen a cloud covering that warded off the most bitter of the cold. Temperatures hovered around zero, a vast improvement from yesterday.

"Even though we're continuing to follow up on leads in Palmer, we're going to keep on focusing locally," Ben stated. "We know Dezzirae is out there somewhere, and we're all committed to doing whatever it takes to see her safely reunited with her mother."

Jade tried to ignore the glances that passed her way and focused on Ben, wondering if he'd slept at all last night.

"We've got a lot of people this morning," he continued, "both local volunteers and workers from across the state. I'm not here to turn this into a big religious event, but for anyone who feels so inclined, I'd like to offer a prayer for Dezzirae's safe return. If you don't care to join us, there's no pressure or expectations. You can head on upstairs, and we'll meet you there in just a few minutes."

Nobody moved. A moment later, Ben was lifting up his voice to heaven. Aisha and Mrs. Spencer sat on either side of Jade, offering gentle back rubs and hand squeezes that only accentuated how numb she felt. If Ben wanted to pray and others felt like joining him, she wasn't going to argue. But as the morning hours passed without a single word from her daughter, Jade found herself trusting less and less in the power of prayer. If God wanted to bring her daughter home, wouldn't he have done so by now?

Would Dez even be the same child once they were together again? What if she'd been abused? Jade's first encounter with Pastor Mitch wasn't until she was fourteen. How could a child as little as Dez endure anything even remotely similar?

Mrs. Spencer squeezed her hand. Aisha cried softly,

blowing her nose quietly every few minutes. All Jade could think about was that — Christian or not — she'd never forgive God if he let something so terrible happen to her daughter.

CHAPTER 18

Jade's phone rang as soon as Ben finished praying. She started, aware of dozens of eyes on her while she fidgeted clumsily to pull it out of her pocket. The number was blocked.

"Hello?"

Ben hurried beside her. His colleagues crowded around her until she wanted to scream. She wiped one sweaty palm on the leg of her pants and switched the phone to her other hand.

"Jade?"

She knew that voice. "Yeah. Elder Keith? Is that you?" She leaned forward in her seat like that could help her concentrate better on his words. As if she could give him any more of her focus and attention.

"I need to talk to you. I'm on my way to Glennallen now."

Out of the corner of her eye, she saw Ben signal to another one of the troopers. She wished they'd all give her some space. "Where is Dez?" she demanded. "What did you to do her?"

"I can't talk. They might have followed me."

"Who's following you?" It took all her self-control not to scream into the mouthpiece. "Where is my little girl?"

"I'm on the Glenn now. I've just passed Eureka. I can't talk. Reception's terrible."

A wave of static confirmed his words. Jade wasn't willing to lose him. "Keith, wait. Pull over and just talk to me. Tell me what's happened to Dez."

She could only hear every few words. The ones she caught were *Glennallen ... more ... soon.* Just when she thought the phone was about to disconnect, she heard Elder Keith utter a cry followed by the sound of clanging metal.

"Keith!" she shouted again, staring at the men around her. What was going on?

"Keith?" She gripped her cell, her voice pleading. "Keith, are you there?" The call disconnected. She turned to Ben. "What was that? What happened?"

"It sounded like a crash."

"What do you mean a crash? Is he all right?" All the blood drained from her face. "What if he had Dez with him?" The eggs and bacon she ate for breakfast sloshed around angrily in her stomach.

Ben's face was somber. "You know about as much as we do right now. Give me a few minutes to figure out our next step."

"What do you mean figure out your next step? He said he was just passing Eureka. We need to drive out there and find him."

"Just give us a minute." Ben retreated with some of the other officers, leaving Jade with Aisha and Mrs. Spencer and their smothering attempts at comfort. Jade didn't need soothing words or well-meant hand squeezes. She needed answers.

"You know God works everything out for good." As soon as the words left Mrs. Spencer's mouth, Jade wanted to throw up. She couldn't take it anymore. How could you say that to a mother whose daughter was missing? What if Dez had been in the back of Keith's car when he got into a wreck? There were no hospitals between here and Eureka. Aside from the small Glennallen clinic, the nearest hospital set up to handle emergencies was back in Palmer. She couldn't waste the day waiting, trying to guess what might have happened.

She stormed over to Ben. "I'm coming with you."

He looked surprised. "What's that?"

"You're going to Eureka to see if you can find Keith,

right? And I'm coming with you."

He took her gently by the elbow and led her away from his little huddle of officers. "I don't think that's a good idea. We have no idea what to expect when we get there."

"This is my daughter." She clenched her fists. "You heard that phone call. You heard how it ended. Something happened on the road, and I'm not going to sit on my bum waiting to hear from you."

"Fine." Ben mumbled something to one of the other troopers before facing Jade once more. "You can ride with me. Come on. We're on our way now."

CHAPTER 19

"You really think it's a good idea to go with him?" Aisha asked as Jade pulled on her coat.

"I don't care if it's a good idea or not. I'm going to find my daughter." The sun was just starting to rise. The volunteer teams would continue their hunt for Dez here, but Jade was convinced they wouldn't find her. There wasn't any reason for Jade to stay in Glennallen. Elder Keith, if not the actual perpetrator, was involved in Dez's disappearance. She had to get to him. Had to find out what he knew.

Aisha reached out to give her a hug. "I'll be praying for you."

"Thanks." Jade ran her hand over the top of her hair, wishing she had her kerchief to cover up the mess. She hadn't looked in a mirror all morning, which was probably a good thing.

"You ready?" Ben asked, tucking his radio into his pocket.

She nodded, grateful that he'd agreed to take her with him. She still needed time to absorb the details he'd shared earlier about his father's death, but she knew she trusted him. He might be the only man in a uniform she did trust at the moment, but it was nice to feel like she had an ally.

"My car's right out here."

She followed him silently, trying to remember exactly how many miles it was to Eureka, whether that was before or after the part of the Glenn Highway with that steep drop-off. Last summer, one of the other daycare workers was run off the road and had suffered quite a few injuries. It would be even worse in the winter, where the dangerous temperatures and short daylight hours made rescue attempts all the more difficult.

Ben opened the passenger door for her, a strange gesture Jade hadn't been expecting. "Thank you," she mumbled.

"Mind if I put on some music?" Ben asked when he was seated beside her.

Jade could only guess what kind of music a white Alaskan state trooper would listen to and hoped it wasn't country. He pulled up a playlist on his phone, a contemporary gospel soundtrack. Jade had no complaints.

Soon they were on the road, following a caravan of

officers.

"So you're new to Glennallen?" she asked after the first song ended.

Ben nodded. "I spent a few years as a public safety officer in Kobuk, then I was ready for a change from bush life and ended up here."

Jade figured the polite thing, the expected thing, would be to ask for more details. *What made you decide to go into law enforcement? What was it like working in the bush?* But she remained silent and stared at the spruce trees, spindly, sickly looking things that stretched out for miles on either side of the highway.

"What about you?" Ben finally asked. "How long have you been in Glennallen?"

"Four years now," Jade answered, and since it would be another hour or longer to Eureka, she told him more. About the heart attack that killed her mom shortly after her dad's murder. About needing to get away from Palmer, away from the memories.

"It sounds bizarre," she admitted, "but every Sunday after Dad died, I'd lay awake and wonder if I should go to Morning Glory. They were the only church I knew. We were family."

She glanced at Ben, wondering if he'd tell her how

stupid she sounded. Who would ever be tempted to go back to a congregation like that?

"I can understand. In a way." His voice was slow. Thoughtful. "After my dad died, my mom started dating this real idiot. Lazy alcoholic, real piece of trash."

Jade tried to keep a neutral expression.

"He was abusive almost from the beginning. Not toward me or my sister," Ben added, "but he threatened my mom nearly every day. He'd push her around, but she always made it out like it wasn't that bad. Like since he never used his fists, it was totally justified. I hated that man, couldn't stand the sight of him, and I didn't get why my mom just wouldn't leave him. Well, she tried. Once. She found out he was cheating on her, and we moved out, but two weeks later he was knocking at our apartment door telling us how sorry he was and begging for a second chance. She gave it to him. And a third chance. Then a fourth.

"My sister Beth was out of the home by then, and I moved in with her my senior year of high school. Just couldn't stand seeing Mom put up with that jerk. For a while I thought if I stuck around, I could keep an eye on her. Protect her. Maybe try to talk her into leaving. Then I finally came to realize she was never going to walk out. He told her so many times she was fat or she was ugly or she was stupid, and he was always railing on and on about how lucky she was to have him because no other man in his right mind would ever love her, and I think after listening to those lies long enough she started to believe them."

Jade had never compared her relationship with Morning Glory to one with an abusive partner, but the metaphor fit.

"Interestingly," Ben went on, "my sister's also the victim of spiritual abuse." He used the term so freely that Jade didn't want to admit she'd never heard the phrase before.

Another perfect fit.

"She went to UCLA for their elementary ed program, and she got tied up in this Christian campus group. I went with her a couple times. Really dynamic group. Amazing worship music. I can see why she was drawn in. But the teaching got really skewed. First it was all about how God wants all his children to be rich and prosperous, and I know there are lots of churches who emphasize that, but these were nearly all college students living in studio apartments eating Ramen every night, and they were being fed these lies by this super sleazy pastor who drove a brand-new Jaguar and gave himself a full spa treatment every week. So he's making my sister and her friends feel guilty because they're not *praying in the blessings* like he put it. But then it got even worse.

"He got so focused on material riches that he told everyone they had to stop shopping at thrift stores. That God said he wanted them all to be *the head and not the tail*, so they couldn't wear secondhand clothes. I mean, who's ever heard a sermon about where college students can buy their hoodies from, right?

"The worst part was they had this whole discipleship program, which sounds all impressive, but it went way overboard. Everybody in the church was supposed to have a discipler. It's basically a mentor, which is a decent idea except these kids like my sister were relying on their mentors for things like telling them what major to declare or what internships to apply for. And it wasn't asking them for advice either. You needed your discipler's permission to do just about anything. And you don't even want to get me started on the whole dating part of it. First of all, if you were interested in someone, you had to confess that to your discipler right away. And it had to be someone from that same campus group or it was just a temptation straight from the devil to distract you. And then your discipler would pray, and if they thought God was telling them to, they'd approach that other person's discipler and basically make it into this whole matchmaking ordeal. Talk about creepy.

"I went to a meeting once with my sister where a college sophomore went up on stage and confessed that she and another boy from that same church group had gone on a date without getting their disciplers' blessing, and even though they got along really well, she knew God was telling her to call it off because she'd been unsubmissive."

Jade didn't reply. It sounded so similar to the schemes at Morning Glory, but she had a hard time picturing the same degree of control being exerted in other congregations as well.

"The really sad part," Ben went on, "was that this group had a lot of great things going for it. The preacher was really gifted in evangelism. He started the group my sister's freshman year, and by the end of that first semester, something like fifty or sixty students had gotten saved. Even for a big school like UCLA, that's amazing. It could have been great, but somewhere in there the gospel got confused with this bizarre discipleship mentality. It was a real shame."

"How did your sister get out of it?" Jade asked.

"Beth? She didn't. She's still living in LA, still going to that same church. They've expanded from just college ministry now, although that's still one of their primary focuses. They've got this huge lot set up in Hollywood, big gaudy church right in the middle of the projects down there, and they're still doing their thing."

"Is she happy?" Jade hoped her voice didn't sound too wistful.

"Happy?" Ben shrugged. "I assume so, although if she wasn't, I'm not sure how she'd manage to tell me. But she's doing well. She gave up on education and is now some executive type for this talent agency. She's making bank, just like her pastor told her she should be. She had a discipler at UCLA, and one morning this woman called her up and said she had a dream that Beth married this dude from their church, so now they're together and expecting their second kid. All that from one dream."

Jade hadn't prepared to spend the entire drive talking, but she found herself telling Ben about Lady Sapphire. "It was the same thing with our pastor's wife. If she had a dream, no matter what it was or how weird it sounded, people believed it."

"Sounds a lot like what my sister went through. What kind of dreams did this Lady ... what was her name again?"

"Lady Sapphire."

"Yeah. What kind of dreams did she have?"

Jade stretched back her memory. "All kinds. Once she had a dream that this girl who was a few years older than me was trying to seduce one of the elders. She made her come up to the front of the church and confess her sin, and then they all anointed her and laid hands on her to cast out the spirit of lust. Another time there was this guy at our church who was bidding on a construction job, and she told him she had a dream where a demon was sitting on the site of the new project, so he withdrew his bid, and then it came out that the business went bankrupt and they wouldn't have been able to pay him. So sometimes it actually seemed like it came true."

"Did she ever say anything or have a dream that turned out to be false?"

Jade told him about Lady Sapphire's dream of a child to carry on her husband's ministry. "Even into her forties, she had the elders anointing her and praying over her all the time so she could have this child. I don't know what she's said about it now that Pastor Mitch is dead."

Jade stopped as a sickening, sloshing feeling returned to her stomach.

Ben glanced over at her. "Something wrong?"

She couldn't respond.

"Did I upset you bringing up all the stuff about your

church?"

"What? No, it's not that. I was just thinking." She let her voice trail off.

"What is it?" he asked. "Is it about your daughter?"

Her body shuddered as she let out a sigh. "I was just thinking. Lady Sapphire thought God promised Pastor Mitch a child to carry on the Morning Glory ministry, but he never managed to get her pregnant. What if she's decided Dez is the answer to that dream of hers? What if she thinks Dez is destined to fulfill that prophecy?"

Jade watched Ben's throat constrict as he considered her words, but he didn't have time to answer before a voice came over his radio. Jade heard the words, but the static and the pounding of her pulse in her ears made everything difficult to understand.

"What was that?" she asked when Ben put the radio down. "Is it Elder Keith?"

This time, it was Ben's turn to sigh loudly. "Yeah, they found his car down the side of the bluff. Major wreck."

Jade held her breath. "Was Dez in there with him?"

"No, and it's a good thing too. The car's completely destroyed. Nobody could have survived."

"Does that mean ..." Jade had a hard time finishing her thought.

Ben nodded. "Yeah. Keith Richardson is dead."

CHAPTER 20

They arrived at the site of the crash about fifteen minutes later. Jade could see the tire tracks in the snow where the car ran off the road, but the crash site itself was too far down. "You wait here," Ben told her. "I'm going to meet the team to see what they've found in the car."

"What are you looking for?"

"Anything that could give us a clue why he was on the road to meet you or what he knew about your daughter's disappearance. May as well tell you now that they've suspended the search back in Glennallen. The message just came through. This has turned into an official abduction case."

Jade blinked, hardly registering his words. All she knew was that Keith Richardson had answers, but now he was dead.

What had God been thinking?

"Are the roads really icy?" she asked. "Was it an accident?"

Ben sighed. "Your guess is as good as mine right now. That's another reason I want to get down. Just wait up here." He pulled the keys out of his pocket. "You can run the car if you get cold. I'll come up as soon as I know anything. Do you have phone reception here?"

She checked her cell. "No."

"Okay, I didn't think so. I'll come back to fill you in as soon as I can, all right?"

Jade nodded. She felt like she owed Ben a thank you or an apology or something. She was just too confused to figure out why.

Sitting in the passenger seat of his car, she thought through everything she knew. Elder Keith wanted to get in touch with her. He was trying to tell her something about the case. If he'd kidnapped Dez for revenge or ransom, wouldn't he have said so? Dez wasn't in the car with him, thank God, but he was speeding to Glennallen to tell Jade something. What?

And was he going so fast that he lost control on the wintery roads and crashed down the ravine? It was possible. Jade always hated driving this stretch of the Glenn Highway, with its steep embankment and sharp turns and no guardrail in sight.

But what if someone else — someone who didn't want

Keith to tell Jade what he knew — was responsible? What if they'd messed with his car or drove him off the road or …

But who would do that? And if Keith hadn't kidnapped her daughter, who had?

Faces and nameless images clashed around chaotically in her mind, and she realized she was hungry. Apparently even a breakfast as hearty as Mrs. Spencer's didn't do a whole lot after a night spent tramping around outside in the snow looking for her missing five-year-old.

Jade squeezed her eyes shut, visualizing for a moment a nice peaceful morning at home with her daughter. No sore feet, no aching back. Just her and Dez eating breakfast, watching a few silly animal videos on YouTube …

The passenger door flew open. She turned her head in time to see a figure dressed in black, pointing a gun at her through the window.

She didn't have time to scream.

Searing pain splintered through her skull.

Then there was nothing.

CHAPTER 21

"Come on, Jade. I know you're in there somewhere. Wake up." The sweet, melodic voice pulled Jade out of her pain-free slumber. The flickering lamp in the corner seemed as bright as Alaska's midnight sun on the summer solstice. Her head throbbed, and her eyes hurt.

She felt dizzy and almost threw up when she turned toward the figure beside her.

"Good."

Jade could hear the smile in the woman's voice even through the ski mask she wore.

"Do you know who I am?"

Did she? Did she know anything? Jade tried to remember where she was or what she was doing lying on the wooden floor in a strange room.

The woman raised her long, elegant fingers and removed the mask. "Now do you recognize me?"

Jade knew that her body was supposed to respond, that she was supposed to feel afraid.

"I hope Gabriel wasn't too rough with you. Was he?" A second figure, also in black, emerged from the shadowy corners, standing guard behind Lady Sapphire.

Her smile was like a snake's. "So sorry about your head. But I assure you that you'll be fine."

Jade reached up to rub her skull, but Sapphire grabbed her by the wrist. "Not right now, darling. You're lucky Gabriel didn't crack your skull open. He's stronger than he looks, my dear, which is saying quite a bit, isn't it?"

She let out a mirthless chuckle.

"Now, tell me, are you going to be a good girl, or are we going to have to deal with you just like we did with Elder Keith?"

Jade blinked, begging her mental processes to speed up. This wasn't the time to feel groggy or light-headed. She had to figure out where she was, and then she needed to escape.

"If you're looking for Gabriel's gun, I assure you we have no more intentions of shooting you now than we did back in that trooper's car. Let's cooperate, shall we? For old time's sake."

Jade squeezed her eyes shut as if she could will away the pain on the top of her head.

Sapphire ran the back of her fingernails up and down

Jade's arm as if she were trying to tickle her. Jade tensed her entire body.

"No need for that." Sapphire clucked her tongue disapprovingly. "The way I see it, you owe me an apology. After all those lies you spread about my husband, did you think I was just going to forget all about you?"

Jade forced herself to sit up, surprised when neither Sapphire nor her henchman made a move to stop her.

Instead, Sapphire smiled. "That's good. I knew you'd be feeling better soon. Once that goose egg dies down, you'll be as good as new."

"Where's Dez?"

"The child?" Sapphire widened her eyes in mock surprise. "Didn't I already tell you? She's in the next room."

Jade made a move to stand, but she was far too slow. Before she even got to a crouch, Gabriel had his arms wrapped around her waist and Sapphire held her finger to her lips. "Shh. The little one's sleeping. She had quite the eventful night, I can assure you."

Jade flung herself from once side to the other, but she couldn't break free. "Dez!" she tried to scream before Gabriel smothered her face with his beefy palm.

"We can't have any of that now," Sapphire scolded.

"Didn't I just tell you she needed her sleep?"

"What did you do to her?" Jade kept her voice low to avoid getting suffocated again by Gabriel's massive hand.

"Told her the truth." Sapphire's smile widened. "All of it. Imagine how surprised I was to discover the child didn't even know who her father is."

"God's her father."

Sapphire nodded patiently as if Jade were the same age as Dez. "That's what she said. But don't worry. She was quite happy to learn that she had a real daddy who loved her very much."

"You won't lay a hand on her."

Sapphire shrugged. "Think what you will. It means nothing to me one way or the other."

"What do you want?" Whatever game this was, Jade was sick of it. If Sapphire was telling the truth, if Dez really was sleeping in the next room, Jade just had to bide her time and wait for the chance to make her escape. Gabriel had a gun, which meant that if he wanted her or her daughter dead, they would be by now. Jade simply had to wait. Try to win as much of their trust as she could, wait for them to grow complacent, and then she'd rescue Dez.

It took all her mental stamina to keep from calling out for her daughter, but if Dez really was asleep, it was a mercy that she didn't have to deal with this living nightmare. A nightmare that Jade would bring to an end, just as soon as she got her chance. She was bigger than Sapphire and outweighed her by at least sixty pounds. It was Gabriel she had to watch. Gabriel who had to be convinced she wasn't a threat.

No threat at all.

She glanced at him, trying to figure out where he kept that gun.

Sapphire was standing now, walking around Jade in a wide circle. She glanced at the small window, trying to guess how much longer until the sun went back down. How long had she been unconscious?

The view was blocked by spruce trees. How far into the wilderness had Sapphire taken her?

At least her daughter was nearby. Even though Jade had no proof, she chose to believe that it was true.

The hope of seeing Dez again, the promise of a safe reunion, was all she had to give her strength.

CHAPTER 22

"What's in the bottle?" Jade demanded, eying Sapphire suspiciously.

"Just some anointing oil," she answered. "It'll make your head feel better."

Jade gritted her teeth. "Don't come near me with that."

Sapphire's serpentine smile faded. "Have it your way." She looked over her shoulder and shrugged at Gabriel, handing him the vial then letting out a sigh. "Now, let's have a little chat about what's going to happen next."

Jade was resting on the hard floor with her back against the wall. Sapphire paced while she spoke, but Gabriel kept himself positioned beside Jade the entire time, stationed between her and a door. Was that Dez's room? Jade strained her ears. Could she hear her daughter on the other side? The slightest hint that Dez was nearby would be enough to give Jade the superhuman strength she'd need to take on both her assailants. She was sure of it. She just had to find the right time.

"I'm very sorry for what you went through as a teenager." Sapphire's apology came as a surprise, but she went on without letting Jade speak. "I always knew you had the spirit of seduction, and I'm sorry I didn't bring it before the church when I first suspected it. We would have prayed for you and anointed you and healed you from your sickness. But I had a certain fondness for you, and I'm afraid I let my personal affection for you cloud my discernment. I didn't want to embarrass you, and so I kept my observations to myself. For that I'm truly sorry, and I beg you to forgive me."

Her voice sounded sincere, but there was a haughtiness in her eyes when they met Jade's.

"My husband was a godly, righteous man, the most devout and anointed believer in Alaska, I'm convinced."

Jade wondered if they were talking about the same individual, but again Sapphire didn't give her time to speak.

"His biggest weakness was that he was so compassionate. It's what made him such a Spirit-filled preacher. He had the gift of empathy. He could look at a person and instantly understand what spiritual struggles they were going through. He told me everything about the day you came to him for counseling. Yes, I know all about it, about how that child of yours was conceived. He wanted to help you. He really did. I hadn't warned him about the spirit of seduction I sensed in you. Like I said, I didn't want to expose you to any embarrassment. As a result, my husband fell into temptation."

Jade didn't know what to say. Should she bring up the fact that Mitch's abuse persisted for years before her pregnancy? Should she mention the Bible verses Mitch used to coerce her into compliance, to scare her into silence?

The smile vanished from Sapphire's face, and she stared at Jade with a mix of both pity and contempt. "I want you to know that I forgive you. I know it wasn't you but the spirit of seduction living in you. My husband was a prime target for spiritual attack given his success in the ministry, so it's no wonder the devil decided to oppress him in this way. At first, I was heartbroken. Devastated that my husband would fall like this. But then one night, God gave me a dream. He showed me a picture of my husband, bent over and weighed down by his guilt and shame. He was chained to prison bars, him and many others, and then just like Paul and Silas in that dungeon, my husband began to sing. His praise released not only his own chains, but those of all the people around him as well. That's when I knew

God was going to exalt my husband to an even higher place of leadership and authority, that he would use my husband's weakness to bring even more children into the kingdom. His prophesies always come true."

Something changed in Sapphire's countenance. "And speaking of prophesies," she went on, staring at Jade with the intensity and beady eyes of a cat, "let's talk for a minute about your daughter."

Jade glanced over at Gabriel, trying to figure out how many seconds she'd have to wrap both hands around Sapphire's pale throat before he intervened.

"You remember, I'm sure, that God gave me a dream in which he promised my husband a child to carry on the ministry at Morning Glory."

Jade didn't trust herself to respond. It was taking all her energy and focus to keep from killing Sapphire where she stood.

"For decades, I believed the prophesy meant that God would open my womb and give me a child, but I've since learned that his ways are so much higher than our ways, his wisdom so much greater than our own. God never promised that I would be the one to fulfill this promise, but that doesn't mean the prophesy itself could fail. God's calling and plans are irrevocable, and he promised Mitch a child.

Your daughter."

Jade couldn't listen to this crazy woman anymore. She wouldn't. She pictured herself jumping up, charging Sapphire and barging into the closed room to grab Dez, but she remained immobile. What kind of strange mysticism was this? What was this woman doing to her?

Sapphire continued to pace, and Jade was acutely aware of the vibrations she sent through the floor with each step, as if the weight and force of Sapphire's stride had increased tenfold.

"I had a dream a few weeks ago," she began, and Jade clenched her hands into fists. It was the only control she had over her body at the moment.

"In my dream, Mitch had just returned home after a long trip serving God overseas. On his back was an empty sack symbolizing the burdens God had taken off his shoulders during his season of international ministry. His hair had turned white, but his eyes were younger and more joyful than I've ever seen, and as he came toward me, he knelt down on the ground and stretched out his hands, and then this beautiful brown baby girl ran toward him shouting, 'Daddy! Daddy! You're home!' and he hugged her and promised he was never going to leave her again.

"I woke up, and I could still feel the love and the joy

that surrounded my spirit in that reunion, and I knew what the Lord was telling me. I wasn't the one he chose to bear Mitch a child to complete his life's work and calling, but I could see the prophesy fulfilled nonetheless. It was a glorious picture. The next night, I had the same dream, except after that little brown girl ran into Mitch's arms, she turned to me and smiled and said, 'I love you, Mommy.' And that's when I knew what God was calling me to do."

Jade felt heavy. Heavy and tired and subdued, as if each word she heard was a chain tying her down. She needed to think, needed all her mental acuity, but she found herself inexplicably drawn to the rhythmic cadence of Sapphire's words.

"I'm sure you're worried about your daughter. That's why I've included you in my plan. That and the fact that Elder Keith wasn't strong enough to do what had to be done. He was with us at first but then changed his mind. He'll receive his reward, I'm sure. Now the biggest question is up to you. Will you be reunited to our fold? Will you come back under the congregational headship God has called you to? Think of what a glorious testimony that would be when you and your daughter come to live with me under one roof, held fast together by the cords of Christian love. I've talked to your daughter, and I sense a great destiny's been placed over her. What do you say?"

Sapphire stopped her pacing, releasing Jade from her state of transfixed confusion. She leveled her gaze. "I say you're a monster and a freak. You deserve to rot in jail just like your husband should have."

Sapphire frowned, lifted her hands toward heaven, and started mumbling under her breath.

"And stop praying for me," Jade snapped. "I don't want to hear any more about your dreams or your deluded fantasies. I don't want you anywhere near me or my child."

Sapphire's incoherent mutterings grew louder and more intense. The mental fog returned, but Jade strove to break free from its hold.

"You're not a real church," she shouted. "Your husband was a disgusting fraud, and the only power either of you ever had was only because people were terrified of both of you. You pretend to know God's will for others' lives, but you're so crazy you actually think you can get away with kidnapping and murder."

Sapphire chuckled. "Murder? I'm sorry, aren't you the one whose father tried to kill my husband?"

"He didn't want to kill him," Jade replied, even though she wasn't sure if that was the case.

Sapphire raised an eyebrow. "No? Your father was

afflicted with the most oppressive spirit of anger and violence I've ever witnessed. That's why I wasn't surprised to hear what that policeman had to do to him."

Jade jumped to her feet. Sapphire wanted to talk about a spirit of anger and violence? Jade could show her a spirit of anger and violence. She threw her weight into Sapphire, knocking her to the ground as easily as she could have blown out a candle. Straddling her, Jade tried to shrug Gabriel off long enough to land at least one good punch.

Sapphire screamed. "Get behind me, demon."

Jade managed to pry one arm away from Gabriel's grasp and elbowed Sapphire in the gut before slamming her fist into that perfectly upturned nose that always made her pastor's wife appear both haughty and regal.

She couldn't get in any more shots before Gabriel overpowered her, grappling until he had both her arms pinned behind her. She threw her head back but only hit his chest and may as well have been a newborn cub wrestling a lion.

"I wash my hands of you." Sapphire stood clumsily and smoothed down her clothes. "I gave you a chance at restitution." She spat down at Jade on the floor. "And you were a fool to disregard my gracious offer. I wipe the dust off my feet. Everything that happens from here on is your own fault. Your blood is on your own head now."

CHAPTER 23

Jade struggled helplessly in Gabriel's arms while Sapphire took a key from her pocket and opened the door on the far side of the cabin.

"Mama?"

The tiny voice made Jade's pulse surge, and she strained against her confines. Unfortunately, Gabriel didn't seem to be exerting any extra effort keeping her immobilized.

"Dez!" Jade shouted. "Dez! Mama's here!"

Breath and warmth and relief coursed through Jade's entire body when her daughter ran toward her, throwing her arms around her neck. Laughing, Dez ignored the man who kept Jade's arms pinned behind her back.

"Mama, Auntie Sapphire says she knows where my daddy is and that I really do have a daddy besides God."

"Sweetie, we'll talk about it all later." Jade nestled her head against her daughter's cheeks, soaking in her presence, praising the Lord for allowing her to be with her daughter again. "What have you been doing, honey? Did you get hurt?"

Dez shook her head. "No, I'm okay. Auntie Sapphire told me you were coming, but I didn't think it'd take so long. Why did it take so long, Mama?"

"Mama had a few things to take care of first." She tried hard not to choke on her words. Her heart swelled with love for her daughter, with gratitude for her safety and a simultaneous primal instinct to do everything in her power to keep her safe.

Even kill.

Gabriel was so close behind her she could feel the gun in his pocket. If she could only find the right opportunity …

But that was all secondary. Dez was safe. Keeping her that way was the only thing mattered. She breathed out a silent prayer of thanks, drinking in the sight of her precious child.

Dez put her hands on her hips and jutted out her lip. "Hey, what happened to the top of your head? It's all bumpy."

"Mama got a little owie. It's all right."

"Let me give it a kiss." Dez leaned in and got close enough to Jade's ear to whisper, "I know she's not my real auntie."

Jade's whole body swelled with relief. Of course Dez was smart enough not to be fooled, but she was putting on the perfect act. Jade didn't trust herself to reply to her daughter's words and hoped Gabriel hadn't heard.

"Well, have you been good for Auntie Sapphire?" Jade figured that if her daughter could put on a show, so could she.

Dez's eyes widened in apparent understanding. "Oh, yeah. I had a bit of a hard time falling asleep last night, but then Auntie Sapphire gave me a little pill, and I'm just now waking up."

Jade held back the choke that threatened to well up in her throat. "Well, I'm really proud of you. You've been a big, brave girl, haven't you? Come here and give me one more kiss."

Dez leaned in and whispered, "Don't be scared. I prayed, and Jesus is going to help us."

Jade didn't know what she'd ever done to raise such a perfect, precious, intelligent child. She found herself making God every promise imaginable, all the ways she'd be a better mom if he would only get them both out of this situation. She knew where Gabriel's gun was, but she had to wait for the right time. After her father's murder, Jade had taken several handgun classes, vowing to never let herself meet the same kind of fate as her father had. Other women in her class wondered if they'd have the fortitude to actually take a life if necessary, but with her daughter's freedom and safety at stake, Jade had no qualms.

"I love you so much, baby," she told her daughter. "And Mama's so, so proud of you."

CHAPTER 24

"Hey, what's that for?" Dez asked when Sapphire came in from the back room carrying a long rope.

Sapphire smiled sweetly. "Well, darling, do you remember that talk we had last night? About how some people have those big, mean demons who want to make them do bad things?"

Dez widened her eyes and nodded.

Sapphire handed the rope to Gabriel and continued to talk as if she were a Sunday school teacher telling her students about Jonah and the storm. "Well, sometimes those big, mean demons have to get prayed out of people, and sometimes when that happens they make them do mean things, like try to fight off the ones who want to help them. So the rope's to make sure your mommy doesn't hurt herself when we pray the demons out of her."

Dez crossed her arms and pouted. "What makes you think Mama's got demons?"

Jade tensed. Wished she could find some way to

communicate with her body. Dez was doing such a good job playing the role of the obedient, compliant child. She had to keep it up if they wanted to get out of this alive.

Sapphire's voice was patient and melodic. "Well, your mom's angry. She's got a lot of hurts about a lot of things, and we want to pray to make her all better. But sometimes this kind of praying we're going to do makes people get angry first, so we're just going to use this rope to make sure she doesn't hurt herself or anyone else."

Jade's mind was working five times as fast as normal. As long as it was a human constraining her, she had a chance of escape. If Gabriel got complacent or distracted, she could make her move. A rope didn't have those kinds of weaknesses she could exploit.

Get closer to the door, she tried to tell her daughter. Why couldn't telepathy work? *Move closer to the door, baby.*

At this point, Jade knew that hoping for her safety as well her daughter's was too much to expect. She just needed to give Dez a chance to run. Jade had no idea where they were, if they were still near Eureka or not, but it wasn't dark out yet, and if they were surrounded by woods, Dez could get away.

That was the goal.

Get closer to the door, baby.

Dez was still staring at the rope and ignoring her mom.

Sapphire took a step closer, her face hardening as she addressed Jade. "Remember now, I gave you the chance to do this the gracious way, and you turned it down." She draped the rope around Jade's shoulders like a scarf.

"What are you doing to Mama?" Dez demanded. With her eyes, Jade tried to calm her daughter's fears. Tried to communicate what she needed to do. *Get by the door, baby.*

Dez took a step backwards. One step closer to the exit. To freedom.

Good job, baby.

Jade tried to give her daughter an encouraging nod, and while Sapphire tied a knot in the rope, Jade kept her eyes on her daughter, praying she could understand.

By the door, baby. Keep going. I love you. You're going to be okay.

The knot was complete. Jade couldn't wait much longer.

Sapphire leaned down to tighten the noose. "Don't make this any harder on your daughter than it has to be," she whispered.

Now.

Jade kicked Sapphire in the groin, splaying her

backwards. "Baby, run!" she shouted. She turned around as Gabriel pulled out his gun. She tackled him onto the floor, grabbing his wrist with all her strength.

He wrapped one leg around her, trying to knock her off balance. Jade held fast. She couldn't see if Dez had fled or not, but there wasn't time to check. If she lost her grip, she was dead.

Letting out an animalistic grunt, Jade held onto Gabriel's wrist, trying to slam his hand on the ground to make him lose his grip. The flickering lamplight glinted off his eyes, and she knew what she had to do. It was her only hope. She gouged one of his eyes with her free hand, turning her brain off so she didn't have to register the feel of it.

He screamed. The distraction had worked.

Jade grabbed the gun.

There wasn't time to think. If she stopped to think, she might change her mind. Might not have the courage.

She aimed. Braced herself for the deafening burst, the powerful kickback. Gritted her teeth in determination.

Jade pulled the trigger.

CHAPTER 25

There wasn't time to look back. Jade had to find her daughter.

She stumbled out the cabin door, praying to reach Dez before anybody else did. Sapphire had fled the cabin while Jade was fighting Gabriel, which meant she could be anywhere. Jade had to be ready.

And she had to protect her daughter.

She screamed Dez's name, uncertain if she was making noise or not because she couldn't hear anything, not the crunching of snow beneath her feet or the sound of her panting or frantic yells.

"Dez!"

Previously, during the fighting, her vision had blurred. Narrowed. Now, her periphery slowly returned to focus. "Dez!"

She scoured the snow for tracks. Where had her daughter gone?

Jade still had the gun. Gabriel would never come after

her again, but Sapphire might. She had to hurry. Had to get to her daughter before that woman did.

"Dez!"

There inside some ATV tracks were footprints small enough to be her daughter's. Racing ahead, she stumbled through the snow heaves until she caught sight of a tiny bundle making her way down the trail. "Dez!"

Her daughter turned around, running toward her. As she came near, Dez's tear-streaked eyes danced with joy. Jade bent down to embrace her.

"I'm sorry, Mama," Dez was sobbing. "I knew I shouldn't go with that lady last night, but she said she knew my daddy, and she seemed awful nice at first. But I was really bad to go with her. Please don't be mad at me."

Jade's tears mingled with her daughter's while they hugged in the snow. "Shh. It's over now. Everything's going to be okay."

"So we're safe?" Dez asked.

Jade wiped the tears off her daughter's cheeks. The last thing Dez needed was for them to freeze to her face.

"We're going to be."

"I didn't know which way to go." Dez was still crying softly. "I didn't want to get lost, but you told me to run, and I didn't want to disobey you again, so I just went."

Jade looked down. Dez's pants were covered in snow and ice. She had to get them someplace dry.

"Do you know which way we should go?" Dez sniffed.

Jade's first instinct was to get them both as far away from that cabin as possible, but she had to be more logical than that. She had no idea what time it was, but the sunlight wouldn't last much longer. Neither of them had coats, and Dez was already shivering. Jade took off her oversized sweatshirt and wrapped her daughter up.

"What about you, Mama? What are you gonna wear?"

"Don't worry about me. It's my job to worry about you."

She took her daughter's hand and looked around, trying to gauge by the position of the mountains which direction they needed to walk.

"Are you mad at me, Mama? For going with a stranger last night?"

Jade shook her head. "Don't be silly. Of course I'm not mad. I'm so happy to find you safe and sound I could give you about a million kisses right now."

Dez grinned. "Oh, yeah? Prove it?"

Jade didn't waste her time arguing.

CHAPTER 26

"Mama, how long do you think we've been walking?"

"Shush, baby, and let me think."

"But my legs are sore, and I'm freezing."

"Stop whining, and hush for a second." Jade paused to study the mountains. She'd been certain that as long as she kept them to her back, she'd end up at the Glenn, but it was twilight now, and there was still no highway in sight.

"Listen, baby, when those bad people brought you to their cabin, how'd they get you there?"

"What do you mean?"

"I mean, did you walk or take a snow machine or a car or what?"

"It wasn't a car. It was a truck."

"Okay. And when you were driving in the truck, before you turned to get to the cabin, where were the mountains? Were they on this side of you or were they somewhere else?"

Dez pouted. "Which mountains do you mean?"

"The big ones, baby." Jade noted the irritation in her voice and tried to soften it. "The big mountains," she repeated more gently. "I want you to think. Were the mountains over here like this?"

Dez shrugged. "I don't know."

Jade let out her breath. It wasn't her daughter's fault. None of this was her daughter's fault. In fact, if Jade had been more open in talking to Dez about her biological father to begin with, none of this would have happened.

"Mama, are you mad at me?"

"What? No, baby." Jade leaned over to give her daughter a comforting hug. "Mama's just trying to figure out which way we need to get to. That's all."

Dez scrunched up her nose. "Are we lost?"

Jade mulled over her next words. "No, baby. I just need to get us to the highway. That's where we'll find some help."

"Well, how long until we get to the highway? I'm hungry."

"I know, baby. This is all gonna be over real soon. And then we'll stop for something to eat. I think there's a lodge in Eureka. We'll get nice big bowls of hot soup. Doesn't that sound good?"

"I want a burger," Dez announced with a pout.

"Fine. You can get a burger and a bowl of hot soup."

"Will they have ice cream?"

"Too cold for ice cream, baby."

"Yeah, but last night you said you'd get me ice cream."

Jade had forgotten all about that. "Fine. Tell you what. Once we get to that lodge, we'll ask if they have ice cream and if they do, you can have as many bowls as you can finish off."

"Promise?"

"Promise."

Dez revived a little at the prospect of food and sweets, and she walked for a while without complaining.

"Hey, Mama?" Dez finally said as the sun made its last faint glimmer on the horizon.

"What, baby?"

"Is anything that lady said true? Was my daddy really a pastor in Palmer?"

Jade could think of a thousand other topics she'd rather be discussing. "Well, baby, he called himself a pastor, but he wasn't."

"Then what was he?"

How was Jade supposed to answer that? Was she supposed to tell her child that her own father was a criminal? A serial rapist and child molester? "He's

123

someone God loves, but he did a lot of bad things and hurt a lot of people, so I don't want you to worry about him none, you got that?"

Dez seemed to consider her words. "Did you love him?"

The question surprised her. Where did her child come up with these crazy notions? "No. I didn't love him. I trusted him, but it turned out I shouldn't have. He was dangerous."

"Kind of like Auntie Sapphire?"

"Right. Like Auntie Sapphire."

"She isn't my real auntie, right?"

"No, baby. She's nothing to you. Nothing at all."

"I didn't think so."

They kept on walking, and Jade let out a silent prayer for help. She was doing everything in her power to stay calm and composed for her daughter's sake, but she had no idea what she'd do if the sky went black while they still were out here lost in the woods.

"Hey, Mama?" Dez finally asked.

Jade sighed. "What, baby?"

"Was my daddy handsome?"

Jade tried hard not to laugh. Pastor Mitch handsome? "I suppose some people thought he was."

"Did you?"

"No. No, I didn't. But I think his daughter's the most beautiful out of all of God's creations."

Dez wasn't deterred by the flattery. "Was he black like you or white like Auntie Sapphire?"

"He was white, baby, but it doesn't matter, okay? God made you just the way he wanted you to be."

"Is that how come you didn't like him? Because he was white?"

Jade needed God's help to get her daughter of the cold woods alive, but she also needed his help to keep her patience. "There's lots of white men I like. Color of their skin has nothing to do with it. Your father did some bad things, things that you don't need to know about. But God loved him, and that's all that matters, okay?"

"Will I ever meet him, do you think?"

"I don't think so, baby," Jade answered. "I don't think so."

CHAPTER 27

"Why are we stopping, Mama?" Dez's voice was muffled by the heavy mounds of snow surrounding them on all sides. "Don't we have to keep walking to get to the highway?"

Jade had spent the past few hours doing what she could to protect her daughter from worrying, but she couldn't keep up her pretense anymore. "Baby, we've got to stop. I don't think we're going to find the highway tonight, and it's already dark."

"So what are we gonna do?"

"I think we're gonna have to snuggle up real close to stay warm and try to rest here."

"You mean outside?" Dez sounded as incredulous as if Jade had told her that her real daddy was Santa Claus.

Jade tried to keep her inflection positive. "Come on. It'll be fun. Remember last summer when you were begging me to take you camping?"

Dez pouted. "But it's not summer."

126

"No, but we'll think of it as an adventure, all right? And then when you're a little old woman you can tell your babies and grandbabies and great-grandbabies all about the night you slept outside with your mom in the winter, and they'll think you're making it up."

Dez continued to pout. "Well, what's the point of telling them a story like that if nobody's going to believe me?"

"I guess you'll just have to tell them it's true whether they believe you or not."

Jade squatted down with her back against a spruce tree. Its branches were wide enough that they'd kept most of the snow off the ground. She wondered if covering Dez with the spruce needles would help her stay warm.

"It's pokey down here," Dez whined.

"Shh. Let me think for a minute."

Jade situated her daughter between her legs and wrapped both arms around her. "I think you better give me that sweatshirt back," she finally said. "We'll tuck it around us both. Is that okay with you?"

Dez shrugged. "Fine."

"You're a good girl, baby. Did you know that?"

Dez didn't respond. Jade put the sweatshirt back on, thankful that it was large enough she could zip it up with her daughter snuggled against her chest.

"It's a good thing you're my little skinny britches, or else you wouldn't fit. Now you're like a baby kangaroo in its mama's pouch."

She waited for Dez to laugh, but she was silent.

"You okay, baby?"

Dez let out a melodramatic sigh. "Yeah. But next time I say I want to go camping, can we please do it in the summer?"

"Yeah, baby. We can do it in the summer."

Dez fell quiet again, and Jade wondered how she'd ever manage to fall asleep.

"Mama?"

"Yeah, baby?"

"I'm hungry."

Jade squeezed her eyes shut. So many times in her life as a single mom, she'd felt ill-prepared, unequipped to care for a child on her own. So many times she'd had to make sacrifices. Coffee in the morning or money to pay the heating bill. New winter boots for Dez or gas to drive to Anchorage where groceries were cheaper. There was that time she got behind in her rent because Dez caught strep throat so they were out of the daycare for a week. Jade had gone whole days eating nothing but a can of beans. But that whole time, no matter how bad things got, her daughter had never missed a meal.

Help me, God. I can't do this.

Jade still wasn't sure if resting here was the best idea or not. What if Dez drifted off to sleep and never woke up? But Jade was exhausted, and the longer she walked around in the woods in the dark, the more likely she was to get them even more lost. No, the best thing was to stay put. Was anyone out here looking for them? She hadn't thought about Ben all night, but he must be searching for her. She prayed God would lead him to this part of the woods. Wherever this part of the woods was.

She held her daughter close.

"Mama?"

"Yeah, baby?"

"That guy who was holding you, he was a bad guy, right?"

"Yeah, baby. He was a real bad guy."

"Is that why you had to shoot him?"

Jade tried not to show her surprise. "What makes you think I shot anybody, baby?"

"Because I heard the bang when I was outside running away. And I can feel the gun you've got in your pocket."

Jade squeezed her daughter more tightly. "You're a

129

smart girl. Has anyone ever told you that before?"

"You had to do it, right, Mama? Because he was such a bad guy?"

Jade decided she couldn't avoid her daughter's questions anymore. "Yeah, baby. Mama had to do it."

They sat in silence, a silence that reminded Jade of everything she'd done at that cabin. Everything she'd risked to save this precious little girl, a little girl who might freeze to death overnight zipped up in this oversized sweatshirt.

"Hey, Mama?"

"What, baby?"

"Is God gonna be mad at you?"

"For what? For shooting that bad guy?"

"No. I mean about the demons."

At first Jade didn't know what her daughter was talking about, then she let out her breath. "Oh, baby, that was just a whole bunch of nonsense. That woman was crazy. I don't want you to think about a single word she said, okay?"

"Yeah, but did you really have demons making you do bad things?"

"No, silly. Of course not."

"Are demons real then?"

Jade would have loved to talk about nearly anything

else, but she knew Dez was stubborn enough she would just keep on asking until she got her answer.

"Yeah, baby. There's demons. But the Bible says God's stronger than all of them, so it's not something you need to spend a lot of time worrying about."

"Do you think demons make me do any of the bad things I do?"

Jade was surprised. "What kind of bad things are you talking about?"

Dez lowered her voice and leaned into her mom. "Well, once at daycare I told one of the Cole twins she was stupid. I know it's a bad word, Mama, and I felt really sorry for it afterward and even gave her my Twinkie at snack time. I don't even know why I said it. We were just playing together is all, and I wasn't even mad, but I looked at her and said that. Think it was a demon in me making me say such a bad word?"

"No, baby. Demons can't live in people that way, not people who belong to the Lord."

"Do we belong to the Lord?"

"Of course we do. Remember when you were down in Sunday school with Mrs. Spencer and you asked Jesus to forgive all your sins and teach you how to live a good life?"

"Uh-huh."

"Well, that means you're a Christian, baby, and demons can't live in Christians. So I want you get all that nonsense out of your mind. It was just crazy talk from a crazy woman."

"Do you think Auntie Sapphire has demons, Mama? Is that why she did all those bad things to us?"

"I don't know, baby. I don't know. Now I want you to try to get a little rest okay? Give Mama a chance to think and figure out what we're gonna do next."

Dez turned and nestled against Jade's chest. Her body relaxed, and her breathing slowed down.

"Hey, Mama?" she said sleepily.

"What, baby?"

"Do you think God really talks to people in dreams like Auntie Sapphire said?"

"I'm sure he does, but I want you to stop thinking about that woman now, you got that?"

"Okay, but I was just wondering, what if we pray and ask God to give us a dream to tell us how to get out of the woods?"

"You go ahead and pray that, baby. Mama's too tired."

"But if I pray it, do you think he'll answer?"

"You go ahead and pray, and I'll listen in, okay?"

Jade shut her eyes and listened to her daughter's

confident prayers. Her five-year-old trusted God to give her a dream to lead them out of the woods. But all Jade hoped was to stay warm enough that they'd both be alive when morning rolled around.

CHAPTER 28

"Mama! Mama! It worked!"

Jade forced her eyes open. Had she been asleep? "What worked, baby?"

"My prayer. When I asked Jesus to give me a dream."

Jade waited for her brain to snap to alertness. "What are you talking about?"

"Remember when I prayed that God would tell me which way we'd have to go to get out of the woods? Well, he did. I was just falling asleep, and I remembered. I remembered looking out the window when I was in the car with Auntie ... with that mean lady. When we got to the place where the road turned real bumpy, the mountains were behind us. I could see them behind us in the little mirror on the side of my door. I just thought it all of a sudden while I was starting to feel sleepy."

Jade glanced around to see if there was enough moonlight to make out the mountains from here. If Dez was right, then Jade had been walking the wrong way. The

Glenn would be in the opposite direction.

"How long have we been resting here?" she asked, still slightly disoriented.

"Just a minute. I stopped praying, and then I shut my eyes and felt tired. Then all of a sudden, I pictured myself sitting in that car and looking at the mountains behind me."

Jade still wasn't sure if they should try to rest a little more. Without any coats or proper shelter, it was probably safest for them to keep moving, and Dez seemed energized from her answered prayer. Jade, on the other hand, wasn't sure she had the strength.

"I may just need to rest a little more," she muttered.

Dez squirmed in their shared sweatshirt. "But, Mama, I think if God answered my prayers like that to let us know which way we've got to go, then we should follow him and go that way, right?"

Jade sighed. "Yeah, baby. You're right. Let's go." She hated to think about how far they'd headed in the wrong direction and prayed that it wouldn't take them nearly as long to get back to the highway.

"Wait a minute." Dez tugged at Jade's sleeve. "We can't go yet."

"Why not, baby?"

"Because God answered my prayer. Don't you think we

better thank him?"

"Yeah, you're right. You go ahead. You pray, and I'll listen, and then we'll start walking."

A familiar voice from the woods answered, "I'm not sure that's the best idea."

Jade jumped up, spilling Dez out of her sweatshirt. She pushed her daughter behind the trunk of the spruce. "How'd you find us?"

Sapphire shrugged. "Your tracks are all over. It only took me this long because you've walked yourselves in circles. But I knew my persistence would pay off. God honors the patient, right?" She took a step forward. "Now, about my husband's daughter."

"You're not going to lay a hand on her." Jade pulled Gabriel's gun out of her pocket.

Sapphire let out an undignified snort. "You think that will frighten me? You may have turned your back on my husband's church, but you're still a child of Morning Glory whether you acknowledge it or not. And you'd never go against me. I'm your pastor's wife, the first lady of ..."

Jade pulled the trigger. The snow muffled the worst of the echo.

From behind the tree, Dez screamed.

"Stay there, baby," Jade shouted back at her. "Stay right

where you are and keep your eyes shut or you're grounded off the TV for three whole months. You understand me?"

"Yes, Mama."

Jade's body was trembling. She ran behind the tree, scooped up her daughter, and ran. She kept Dez's face covered with her hand until they were far away from Sapphire's body. When she got too tired, she set Dez down and they raced together toward the mountains.

CHAPTER 29

"Over here! We're here!" When Jade saw the search lights in the distance, she scooped up her daughter and started running. Dez had gotten lethargic, and Jade tried to pass on her enthusiasm.

"That's the search team. They're looking for us. Come on."

She followed the light, nearly choking over her joyful laughter. A few minutes later, her daughter was wrapped in a heated blanket, carried in the arms of a search and rescue paramedic. They were a little less than a mile from the highway, and Jade was positive it'd be the easiest hike of her life. Adrenaline propelled her forward. Adrenaline and the need to get her daughter to safety. She begged the man carrying Dez to run on ahead instead of waiting for her. She nearly collapsed into the arms of the other paramedic when she stepped over a major snow heave and the Glenn Highway came into view.

"The ambulance is right down there, ma'am. We'll get you checked out and warmed up."

"I'm not worried about that. I just want to make sure my little girl's all right."

A man in a trooper's uniform stepped up toward her, wearing a familiar smile. "Well, look who finally decided to pop out of the woods."

She tried to match Ben's grin even though she felt ready to die from exhaustion. He wrapped an arm around her, and they walked together to the ambulance where paramedics were already getting Dez warmed up.

"I'm glad you're all right," he said.

Jade didn't know what else to say, and so she lifted up her silent prayers of thanks to God who had delivered her and her daughter once again.

CHAPTER 30

Jade sat in the back of the ambulance next to her daughter's gurney. The paramedics had covered Dez in blankets, and everyone seemed excited that her body had finally picked up its cues to start shivering.

"She's going to be fine," one of the men assured Jade.

The road to the hospital was paved with ice and frost heaves. Jade figured it was probably a good thing that the driver wasn't rushing. He hadn't even turned on his sirens.

"Mama?"

"Yeah, baby?"

"What time is it?"

Jade looked to Ben who was sitting across from her.

"Time to get some sleep." He gave Jade a soft smile.

"Mama?"

"Yeah, baby?"

"We didn't miss Christmas, did we?"

"No, we didn't miss Christmas."

"Good. Because I'm ready to do my lines for the play at

church."

"You are?"

"Uh-huh. *And the angels said, 'Glory to God in the highest, and on earth peace to men on whom his favor rests.'*"

Ben burst into applause. "Very good job. Are you sure you're only five? I know some teenagers who couldn't learn their lines that well."

Dez beamed.

"Thanks again for all the time you spent looking for us." Jade didn't know what else to say. Ben wanted to ride with them in the ambulance so he could talk with Jade about the case, but so far the entire conversation had been focused on Dez and keeping her warm and happy.

Jade couldn't believe their trouble was over, couldn't believe the extent Sapphire had gone to in order to steal her daughter.

"Mama?"

"Yeah, baby?"

"How long we gonna be at the hospital?"

"Not long. We just want to get you all warmed up and make sure you're all right."

Ben leaned forward. "You, too. You're getting checked out just like she is."

Jade shrugged. "I'm fine. The doctor's probably going to tell me all that exercise was good for me."

She caught Ben's eye. When she met him last night, she would have never expected to feel so thankful to have him looking out for her safety. Thankful to have him by her side.

You really do have a sense of humor, don't you, God?

Ben continued to stare at her then cleared his throat. "Well, I guess we should make the best use of the time we've got and compare notes. Let me tell you what I know first."

Jade was happy to let him take the conversational lead.

"We checked out Keith Richardson's car. Someone cut through the brake lines, not all the way but enough to get him to that icy pass and let gravity take care of the rest."

Jade was thankful he spared her any further details.

"We found a letter in his pocket where he talked about how he feared the pastor's wife was the one behind the kidnapping. Said something about her having a dream about her husband's kid … real woo-woo stuff, just like you said. But we compared the handwriting with the note you got earlier. Seems he was trying to help you. Give you some kind of warning. I can show you if you want."

Jade shook her head. "Not now." In fact, she wasn't

sure a letter like that was something she'd ever want to see. "How'd you know where to look for us in the woods?"

"Well, I got back to the car after checking things out at the crash site. Saw a blood splatter on the head rest. Pretty amateur move. We figured Sapphire had you, and we also figured she had someone to help, so we looked into it. Guess there was this Elder Gabriel, some guy who recently moved to Palmer to help run the church. Keith mentioned him in his letter. We looked into it, and it turns out he's got a little cabin near the Sheep Mountain area. We went to check it out, found Gabriel shot and a few kiddie toys in the back room. That's when we brought in the search and rescue team."

He glanced at Dez resting on the gurney. "I'd really like to hear your side of it now, but maybe we should wait."

Jade nodded. There was no need to make her daughter relive every horror and trauma she'd endured.

Dez blinked her eyes open. "You should tell him about the dreams, Mama."

Ben glanced at Jade. "What dreams?"

Dez grew animated. "All kinds of dreams. You should have heard them. Like one about how that lady was supposed to turn herself into my new mom because my dad was the pastor at this church, only Mom says it's not a *church* church, just some weird fake thing. Have you ever been to a fake church?"

Ben shook his head. "Can't say that I have."

"Me either, but if it's got people like this lady, I wouldn't want to go either. I think Mama had the right idea shooting her."

Ben raised his eyebrows, and Jade nodded. So much for trying to protect her daughter from frightening memories.

"Where was that?" Ben asked.

"I couldn't say. Somewhere in the woods. We got turned around."

Dez nodded her head enthusiastically. "Yeah. It was scary. Mom thought we were going to have to spend the night outside even though I've never been camping before because Mom refused to take me last summer when I really wanted to go, and all we had was one sweatshirt for both of us to share, and it was really dark, and Mama got us lost in the woods. It was kind of my fault because I was awake when that bad lady drove me out to the cabin place, only I couldn't tell Mama if the mountains were behind me or to the side or what, so she didn't know how to get us back to the road. And she was getting kind of tired and even a little grumpy." Dez stole a glance at Jade who sat there wondering where her daughter's sudden burst of energy came from.

"Well," Dez went on, "Mama said it was time for us to get to sleep, only I didn't want to spend the night in the cold, and I was hungry too, so I asked Mama if maybe we should pray and ask Jesus to send us a dream to tell us which way to go. Because I figured if that weird church lady had dreams and God talked to her except she didn't even go to a real church, God would definitely talk to us if we asked him nicely, so we did. And then Mama was already starting to snore a little bit, but I wasn't asleep quite yet, only I was about to fall asleep, and I remembered where I saw the mountains in the car, and I knew they were behind me when we were driving. So I told it to Mama, and she said that meant we'd been walking the wrong way, but there was enough moonlight we could see the mountains by then, and if we went toward them we'd find the highway. Which we did but not until we found you guys first."

Ben reached out and ruffled her hair. "You're a good story-teller. Did you know that?"

Dez pouted. "It's not a story. That's how it happened. Tell him, Mama."

"I know it happened," Ben said. "I meant you tell the story in a really exciting way."

"It was a compliment," Jade explained.

Dez glanced at the trooper. "Oh. Well, thank you, officer."

"You're welcome. And on top of being very smart and a good storyteller, you've got excellent manners."

"Oh, that's because Mama says that when I meet a police officer, especially if he's white like you, I've got to be extra polite and make sure …"

"Okay now," Jade interrupted. "I think maybe you should let the grown-ups talk a bit."

"Why? Are you gonna tell him how you shot that big scary guy when that church lady was tying a rope around your neck?"

"Is she making this up?" Ben asked.

"I wish." Jade rolled her eyes. "No, it happened pretty much like she said." Jade started from the point when Sapphire tied her up and explained how they escaped the cabin and ended up in the woods, where eventually Sapphire caught up with them.

"Mama was really brave," Dez inserted. "I don't know if I would have known what to do with a gun because Mama's always telling me I can't go near them or touch them or if I see one lying around I'm never allowed to pick it up and I have to tell someone right away."

"Those are very good rules," Ben said approvingly.

Dez shrugged. "Nah. It's just good sense. Guns are tools, not weapons."

Ben chuckled, which forced Dez into an exaggerated pout. "I wasn't making a joke."

"I know you weren't. I just wish every kid in the state of Alaska were as smart as you are."

She shrugged again. "It's not smart. It's just common sense."

"That's probably because you have a very good mom." Ben glanced over at Jade again, and this time the approval in his eyes was directed at her.

CHAPTER 31

"See you later, kiddo." Ben gave one of Dez's cornrows a playful tug. "Don't you be giving that doctor a hard time, you hear me?"

"Okay, officer."

He leaned down and smiled at her. "Hey, you know what? After all we've been through together, you don't have to call me officer. You can just call me Ben."

"That's *Mister* Ben," Jade added more sternly than she needed to. She turned to him and softened her voice. "Thanks again for all you've done."

"Hey, no problem. That's what I'm here for." He dusted off the front of his perfectly pressed uniform in a gesture that was surprisingly endearing.

Jade tried to figure out what else she could tell the man who helped save her and her daughter's life. "How are you getting back to Glennallen?" It wasn't quite what she meant to say, but at least it was something.

"Pastor Reggie and his family are flying in from their

vacation this afternoon. I'll hitch a ride back with them."

Jade set her hand on her daughter's gurney. "Well, I guess I better go. We've got to get this little girl warmed up."

"Don't forget to let the doctors take care of you too," Ben added, scratching at his cheek.

Jade nodded. "Okay."

"Okay."

She turned to follow the paramedics then stopped. "Oh, Ben?"

"Yeah?"

"Since you're gonna be around town for a little bit, come on by once we get settled in. I can text you what room we're in."

A smile broke across his face, and Jade realized how tired he looked.

"That'd be great."

"I think they have reclining chairs in there too. You know. If you needed a place to crash for a few hours."

"I may take you up on that."

The paramedics had already started to wheel the stretcher down a brightly lit hallway.

"You better go." Ben raised his hand to signal goodbye.

Jade tilted up her chin. A wave with her head. "See you

around." She hurried to catch up with the paramedics.

It was time to focus on her daughter.

CHAPTER 32

After a thorough exam in the ER, a nurse finally led Jade and Dez to the children's wing of the hospital. Jade was fine, just like she'd told every single trooper and paramedic who wanted her to get checked out, but the doctor thought Dez could benefit from warm saline through an IV.

"We could do it here in the ER," he said, "but frankly the pediatric nurses are better equipped at handling such little veins, and I think you'd both be more comfortable."

It wasn't difficult for Jade to agree. The transfer to the children's area was time-consuming, but the nurses on the children's floor were fabulous, and they kept Dez distracted enough while putting in the IV that she hardly fussed at all.

"How long do I got to keep this in?" Dez asked.

Jade yanked Dez's free hand to keep her from scratching the site. "It'll probably just be a few hours. They want to make sure your temperature goes up, and they think you need your rest. Which you do."

"But I'm not tired."

"That's because you like being the center of attention."

Dez pouted. "No, I don't."

"Yes, you do. I saw the way you were hamming it up for Officer Ben."

"He told me to call him *Mister* Ben."

"Well, as long as you're under my roof, you're calling him Officer."

"I'm not under your roof right now."

"Stop being smart with me."

"I thought it was a good thing to be smart."

Jade reached her hand under Dez's pile of blankets to tickle her daughter's ribs. "Too smart for your own good, that's what you are."

Dez giggled, then her face grew more serious. "Mama?"

"Yeah, baby?"

"That church lady, do you think she would have killed you?"

"What makes you say that?"

Dez's whole body heaved as she let out a sigh. "I was just thinking. That's all. I guess it's good you shot them both, huh?"

"No, baby. It's not good. I just did what I had to do."

"Are you gonna get in trouble for it? Is Officer Ben gonna have to arrest you?"

"What? No. They know I did what I had to do to protect my little girl. That's not against the law."

Dez's face twisted.

"What are you thinking, baby? Tell me."

"Did you want to kill them, Mama? Were you mad at them for what they did to us, and that's why you killed them?"

Jade reached toward her daughter and held her while she started to cry. "No, baby. It wasn't like that at all."

"So it wasn't the demons that made you do it?"

"What?" Jade pulled back just long enough to look her daughter in the eyes. "No, of course not. You listen to me. Demons are real, but they don't have any power besides what God gives them. And nobody can make you do anything that goes against God's rules."

"Not even the devil?"

"Not even the devil. I know what happened to us was scary. I'm glad it's over, but it's still really bad that those two people ended up getting shot. God tells mommies and daddies to take care of their kids, just like he tells people like Officer Ben to take care of regular folks like you and me."

"Do you like Officer Ben, Mama?"

Jade shrugged but didn't meet her daughter's eyes. "Sure, I like him. He's a very nice man and good at what he does."

"Would you ever want him to be your boyfriend?"

Jade couldn't keep in her laugh. It felt good to have her daughter talking to her about something as innocent as dating and crushes. "What? Of course not. Why? Do you want him to be your boyfriend?"

Dez giggled.

"Tell you what." Jade picked up the blankets the hospital staff had given her. "Why don't you scoot over in that bed, because these nurses must think you're the size of a baby elephant giving you all this extra room."

"What are you doing, Mama?"

"I'm getting up here and cuddling my baby. That's what I'm doing."

Dez's eyes widened. "Are you allowed to do that?"

"Am I allowed? What do you mean? Are you my child? Did I give birth to you? Do I hug you and feed you and tell you I love you every single day of your life?"

"Yeah."

"Well then, I guess that makes you my baby, and I just happen to think that it's time to snuggle with my baby. Is that all right with you?"

Dez scooted over in the bed. "I suppose."

"Well, thank you very much, Your Highness." Jade gave Dez one last round of tickles and then got busy adjusting the two of them under the blankets. "We'll stay warmer like this, you know."

Dez let out a snort. "Want to hear what I think?"

"What do you think, baby?"

"I think it's just that you don't want to sleep in that chair all by yourself. I think you're too scared."

"You know what, baby?"

"No, what?"

"You're a very smart girl. Have I ever told you that?"

Jade propped herself up on her elbow long enough to watch Dez roll her eyes. "Only, like, every day."

Jade kissed her daughter on the forehead one more time, snuggled up a little closer, and soon was fast asleep.

CHAPTER 33

"Good morning, sunshine!"

Jade groaned at the chipper, perky voice that interrupted her perfectly sound nap. "What time is it?" She blinked at a young woman wearing smiley face scrubs. Nurse Happy pushed a few buttons on the few different monitors and pulled out a thermometer.

"Time for a temperature reading," she announced in a singsong voice.

Jade untangled herself from the blankets and landed back in the reclining chair. She certainly wouldn't win any points for being graceful, but she was far more concerned about the numbers on the thermometer than she was about anything else. "How's she doing?"

The nurse frowned. "96.8. Still not quite as high as we'd like." She reached over Dez and massaged the IV bag. "It's probably time to get this warmed up again. How are you feeling, sunshine?"

Dez blinked up at her. "What are you doing?"

Jade was about to remind her daughter to mind her manners, but the nurse was apparently running on multiple shots from Starbucks and was more talkative than Dez at her most energetic. "We're just checking your temperature. Want to make sure you're strong and healthy so you can go home today. Did you sleep well?"

Dez shrugged. "Mom was snoring in my ear."

"What? I was not."

"Yes, you were. You snore all the time."

"I heard that."

Jade started at the voice and looked over to see Ben standing in the doorway. It was the first time she'd seen him out of his trooper uniform. He looked casual and … nice. Jade wondered where he got the change in clothes. "Can I come in?" he asked.

The nurse slipped past him with a cheerful, "Just holler if you need anything," and bustled out of the room.

Ben walked up to Dez's bedside and set down a shopping bag by her pillow. "How'd you sleep, kiddo?"

"What's this?" she asked. "Is it for me?"

"Dezzirae Rose Jackson," Jade snapped. "Your mama taught you better than that. Where are your manners?"

Dez looked at Jade sheepishly. "Sorry." She turned back to Ben. "What's in the bag, officer?"

He laughed. "Open it and see."

Dez reached over with her arm and pulled out some word searches and animal fact books.

"I figured a smart girl like you would want something to read while you were stuck in bed," Ben said with a smile.

Dez frowned. "I don't know how to read."

Jade crossed her arms. "Did that nurse put rude juice in your IV or something?" she demanded. "When someone gives you a gift," she said sternly, "you tell them thank you."

"Thank you," Dez muttered.

"What'd you say?" Jade pressed.

"Thank you, officer."

Jade let out her breath. "That's better."

Ben leaned toward Jade. "So, how's the patient doing?"

Jade met his gaze with a smile. "Still as stubborn and ornery as ever."

"I think you mean bright and charming, don't you?" he asked, winking at Dez.

"Right," Jade agreed with a slight rolling of her eyes. "That's what I meant."

Ben sat down in one of the stools and stretched out his legs. "Well, I'm glad to know you're both safe. Any word on how long they're keeping her here?"

"We just woke up," Jade admitted, "but from what everyone was saying, we should be released by the afternoon, I'd imagine."

"Need a ride back to Glennallen?"

"Do you have room?"

Ben nodded. "I already texted Reggie. He said they've got enough seats for us all."

"If you're sure it's no trouble."

"Not at all."

Jade licked her lips, suddenly uncertain what she should be doing with her hands.

"Would you like a coffee?" Ben asked after a torturous silence.

"That would be wonderful."

He stood back up. "Got it. Any special way you like it?"

"Strong and black," Dez answered for her, and Jade grimaced when she suspected what her daughter was going to say next. "Just like she likes her men."

"Dezzirae Rose Jackson," Jade hissed.

Dez shrugged her shoulders. "What? That's what you always say when you make yourself coffee at the daycare because the coffee maker we've got at home's broke."

"It's a joke and something that's not fit to be repeated, especially not in front of …" She glanced at Ben, who was standing in the doorway trying not to laugh. "Never mind. But you best start remembering your manners, or I swear with this policeman as my witness I'll tan your hide."

Dez rolled her eyes. "No, you won't. You're just saying that."

"Well, I mean it this time," Jade grumbled, her face still hot with embarrassment.

Ben cleared his throat. "All right. I'll be back in a few minutes with some coffee." He met Jade's eyes and gave her a grin that only deepened her flush. "No cream. No sugar. Just the way God made it."

"I'm sorry," Jade sighed.

He laughed. "Don't worry about it. I like a girl who speaks her mind." He tousled Dez's hair again. "Watch out for your mom while I'm gone. Don't let her get into any trouble."

"I won't." Dez grinned widely.

Ben gave Jade a small wave. "See you soon."

"Take your time." She watched him leave, staring at the empty doorframe until her daughter interrupted with, "Mama?"

"What, baby?"

"Why do you got that goofy grin on your face? Is it because Ben's getting you a coffee? Does that mean the hot policeman likes you?"

Jade snapped her head around. "What'd you call him?"

"Oops, I forgot. I mean Officer Ben. You were staring at him like this." Dez tilted her head to the side, clasped her hands beneath her chin, and batted her eyelashes.

"What?" Jade tried to sound upset but couldn't hide her laughter. "I was not."

"Yes, you were. Is it because you think he's hot?"

"Five-year-old girls don't say *hot,*" Jade told her. "You can say he's handsome, and I guess he is if you like that strong, athletic type."

"He's not handsome, mama. He's hot."

"Dezzirae Rose Jackson!" Jade snapped.

Her daughter shrugged. "Well, it's true."

Jade didn't respond.

"You're doing it again." Dez tilted her head and batted her eyes.

"No, I'm not."

"Yes, you are."

"Read your new book, baby. Mama's tired."

CHAPTER 34

Jade didn't realize how badly she needed a caffeine infusion until Ben mentioned coffee. She hoped he wouldn't be too long and tried to convince herself that her impatience was only because she needed help waking up, not because she was anxious to see him again.

Dez was too perceptive for her own good. The truth was Jade did find Ben attractive, and the more she'd gotten to know him, the more she found herself wanting to spend time with him. Yesterday, she would have told herself that was just the crisis talking. Her world was in shambles, her daughter missing, and Ben could help her find her daughter. But even now that she and Dez were reunited, Jade found herself wondering if she'd see more of Ben in the future. Hoping their paths would cross more often.

It was silly, really. What did she know about him? They went to the same church, and he was a Christian. He'd told her little bit about his past, and in some ways they shared common life experiences. Both had lost their fathers. But in other ways they were the exact opposite of each other and always would be.

It would never work.

She shook her head. She should just be thankful that God had protected her and her daughter and focus on making the time leading up to Christmas as joyful and happy for Dez as possible. She wasn't planning on going all out on gifts this year, but she was going to find money somewhere. Even if all of Dez's toys came from the secondhand store, Jade was going to make sure this was a Christmas she wouldn't forget.

The phone by Dez's hospital bed rang. Jade didn't know if she was supposed to pick it up or not and gave a tentative, "Hello?"

"Hey, it's me."

"Aisha? How'd you find out where we were?"

"I called Ben, and he gave me the hospital room number. Is now a good time?"

"I have a few minutes." Jade eyed the doorway, wondering when Ben would return with those coffees.

"I was so happy to hear you found Dez. Is she all right?"

"Oh, yeah. She's fine. Getting some hot saline in an IV, but her temperature's coming up, and they'll probably send us home today."

"That's great. Will you need a ride or anything?"

"No, we'll be riding back with Pastor Reggie's family and Ben."

There was an awkward pause. "Oh. So is he with you now?"

"He just stepped out to grab some coffee."

Another somewhat stifled, "Oh." Aisha cleared her throat. "Well, we've all been praying for you. Last night, Mrs. Spencer organized a prayer vigil at the church. It was really special. I'm just so sorry you guys went through what you did. Ben said it ended up being your old pastor's wife?"

Jade wasn't sure how much Ben and Aisha had been in touch and resented the small, unwelcome rush of jealousy. Who cared how often two adults decided to talk with one another? He was probably just filling Aisha in so she could pass along any prayer requests to the church. You couldn't blame him for that.

"Tell everyone back in Glennallen thanks for the prayers," she said.

"I will. And hey, I wanted to ask you something about Ben if it's not too awkward."

A nurse stepped into the room and started fidgeting

with Dez's IV bag. "Listen, someone just came in. I've got to go. We'll talk soon though, okay?" Jade didn't know what Aisha had to say to her about the trooper and wasn't sure she wanted to. She hung up the phone and watched the nurse inject a syringe into Dez's IV port.

"What's that you're putting in there?

He cleared his throat. "Just some antibiotics to help with the infection."

Jade frowned. "Nobody said anything to me about any infection."

He kept his face turned slightly, but there was something familiar about his profile.

"That's all here. Got to check on another patient." He gave a weak wave and turned to go.

Jade wanted to stop him. Where had she seen him before? He didn't look like one of the paramedics who transported Dez here.

"Hey."

She watched as he turned around, keeping his gaze focused on the floor.

"Where's our regular nurse?"

He glanced over his shoulder. "She'll be here soon."

Something wasn't right. "I want to talk to the doctor."

He looked relieved. "Sure. I'll go get him."

"Mama?"

Jade turned toward her daughter. "Not now, baby."

"I feel funny."

Jade jumped to her feet and rushed toward the nurse. "Hey, get over here. What did you put in there?"

The stranger started sprinting down the hall. Jade hollered for help. She hated to let him get away, but she wasn't about to leave her little girl. She grabbed the IV, trying to figure out what button would turn it off or how she could stop the flow.

"Help!" she screamed again.

Dez's former nurse ran in. Jade was breathless as she tried to explain, "He put something in the tube then ran away."

The nurse bent down over Dez's hand and disconnected the port. Jade heard a commotion outside but was too busy praying for her daughter, watching as Dez's eyelids fluttered and her head rolled lifelessly to the side.

CHAPTER 35

Jade had never prayed more intensely in her life. Several workers had been called into Dez's hospital room, and Jade was forced to wait outside. Nobody knew what drug the man had injected into her daughter's IV, but it was making her heart rate drop dangerously low.

Jade turned her back to Dez's window. The curtains were drawn, and it was too painful to try to strain her eyes in hopes of making out what was going on.

Please, Lord. You didn't deliver her out of those woods just to let her die here. I'm not ready to lose her.

Jade's whole body was trembling. How much suffering was one little girl supposed to endure before God decided it was enough?

She thought back over every sin, every time she'd lost her temper or yelled at her daughter. Was God punishing her for those things? Had he decided that Jade was an unfit mother, so now he was going to take Dez away?

You know I can't live without her, she prayed. *Maybe*

that means she's become an idol to me, but I can't help that. If you want her with you in heaven, you may as well take me too, because that child is my only reason for living and breathing.

She thought back over all her former plans — college, law school, advancing social justice. Remembering how upset she'd been that her pregnancy derailed each and every one of her goals, she was ashamed now to think she would ever have preferred her education or career over being the mother of this precious, precocious baby girl.

If you want to take her home, Lord, you're going to have to fight me for her.

Even as she prayed the words, Jade knew how stupid they sounded, but she couldn't help herself. If God's only plan was to take Dez away from her, he should have let Sapphire kill them both back at the cabin.

She became aware by degrees of a figure standing next to her. "Is this seat taken?" Ben held out a cup of coffee.

She shook her head.

"I heard about what happened. Do you know what's going on in there?"

She shook her head once more, not trusting her voice to hold.

"The good news is security apprehended the suspect."

She didn't respond. What did it matter, unless the man was willing to tell the doctors what he put in her daughter's IV?

"Want your coffee?" Ben asked.

No.

He sat beside her quietly, and it wasn't until Jade let out a heavy sigh she realized she'd been holding in her breath.

"Should we pray?" Ben finally asked.

Pray? Right now? Did he actually think she'd been doing anything else?

She turned to face him and croaked, "Okay."

CHAPTER 36

"We've got your daughter's heart rate back to a safe range." The doctor poked his head out of the room and held the door open. "Do you want to come in?"

Jade jumped to her feet.

"I'll wait out here," Ben said. "I've got some calls to make anyway."

Jade rushed past the doctor as he explained, "She'll be groggy for a while, but she's going to be fine."

Jade hurried to the bedside and grasped Dez's hand. "You hear me, baby? Mama's here."

Dez's eyes fluttered open. "Mama?"

"Yeah. It's me."

"Mama, I want to tell you something."

"What's that, baby?"

Dez took in a breath that sounded far too labored for a healthy child her age. Jade glanced at the nurses to see if any of them looked concerned. Who would have done this to her baby? Who would have dared?

She squeezed her daughter's hand, praising God for the warmth and life she felt. "You're hurting me," Dez complained.

Jade forced herself to loosen her hold. Dez was lucky there were still so many other people around. Even with the crowd, Jade was half tempted to crawl into bed and smother her daughter in kisses. "What did you want to tell me, baby? I'm right here. The doctors have given you really good medicine, and your heart's going to be just fine and healthy, and everything is under control. You're safe now. So you can tell me anything. What did you want to say?"

Dez opened her eyes wide enough for Jade to see her rolling them dramatically. "I wanted to say that I think you should ask Officer Ben on a date. That's all."

CHAPTER 37

"Well, here it is." Ben stepped into the room, balancing a cafeteria tray in his hands. "A can of soda for the patient, a bowl of soup for Mom, and a fresh cup of black coffee since that first one didn't really go as planned."

Jade took the tray from him. "Thanks so much. Did you get something for yourself?"

"I ate earlier."

Jade didn't want to admit that she was disappointed.

"Sorry it took me so long to get here," he said. "I've been going back and forth with hospital security and the Anchorage police, trying to fill in all the gaps so everyone knows what's going on."

"What is going on?" Jade asked. "I'd like to know myself."

Ben sat on the stool, stretching his legs out from under him. "Well, the guy you saw really is a nurse here, but he's also a member of Morning Glory International. Does the name Caleb Houghton mean anything to you?"

"Houghton?" Jade repeated. "Yeah. Their family was one of the really vocal ones when we went to the police." She didn't say any more.

Ben sighed. "We're still trying to decide if he acted on his own or not."

Jade didn't respond. All that really mattered was that Dez was feeling better. She was safe.

Ben stared at Jade eating a spoonful of soup then leaned down toward the hospital bed. "Hey, kiddo," he whispered, "mind if your mom and I step outside for just a minute?"

Dez drank a sip of Coke from her straw and grinned. "Why? Do you want to kiss her?"

"Dezzirae Rose Jackson," Jade snapped, nearly choking on her food.

Dez shrugged. "It was only a question."

Jade didn't have the courage to meet Ben's eyes. She set her bowl of soup down and followed him out into the hallway. "What's going on?"

He turned to her, his eyes full of seriousness. "I heard from the search and rescue team. They found the spot where you shot Sapphire."

Jade had been waiting for this. Even though it was clearly a case of self-defense, Jade had shot an unarmed woman. She'd also killed Gabriel back in the cabin. That wasn't the kind of thing you could simply walk away from.

"How much trouble am I in?" she asked. "Do I need to find a lawyer?"

He looked confused. "What? Oh, no. That's not it."

"Then what is it?" Her stomach churned at the worried expression on his face.

"It's Sapphire. The rescue team discovered the spot where she fell. They saw the blood, but they didn't find a body. In fact, they were able to follow the blood drops for almost a quarter of a mile."

"What's that mean, exactly?"

"It means Sapphire survived. She's still alive."

CHAPTER 38

Jade wasn't going to believe it. This was some sort of social experiment, where independent film directors with far too much time on their hands set up elaborate hoaxes just to see how people would respond. Somewhere behind her were cameras, a film crew ready to catch her reaction. She wasn't going to give them the luxury of laughing at her for being the world's most gullible person.

"That's ridiculous," she argued. "I shot her myself."

"Did you actually check the body once she fell?"

"I was a little too busy to feel for a pulse if that's what you're asking."

Ben took a step back. "I'm not blaming you. I'm sure there was a lot of stress. It's something anyone could miss."

"I shot her." Jade spoke the words definitively. She could still hear the sound of the gunfire, could see the way Sapphire fell.

"I know you did. And from the looks of it, she lost a lot of blood. But then the trail vanished, and no body has turned up, so we have to assume she survived. We have to be very careful."

"She wouldn't be stupid enough to come after us a second time." How desperate could one woman get?

"I'm afraid she already might have. So far, the nurse in custody isn't talking, but I'm willing to bet she put him up to it. I don't see how else he would have known to tamper with your daughter's IV. Your story hasn't hit the news yet, and he doesn't work on this floor."

What kind of security system did this hospital have if strange men could just walk into a patient's room and inject a child with God only knows what? Jade clenched her jaw. Anything to channel her anger and her fear. Anything to get her mind off Sapphire.

"She can't be alive." Even as she said the words, Jade realized there was no other explanation. "So what do we do now?"

"We tell our guys to keep their eyes open for her. And we give you and your daughter tightened security."

"What's that mean?"

"Well, if it won't make you feel too cramped or uncomfortable, it probably means that you and I will be spending quite a bit more time together."

CHAPTER 39

"Well, we've watched *How the Grinch Stole Christmas, A Charlie Brown Christmas,* and *Mickey's Christmas Carol.*" Is there anything we're missing?" Ben asked.

"I wanna watch *Frozen*!" Dez piped up.

Jade laughed. "I don't really think that's a Christmas movie, baby."

Dez stuck out her lower lip. "But it's got snow in it."

Ben gave a playful shrug. "She's got a point there."

Dez turned to her mom with pleading eyes. "Please?"

Jade stood up. "Fine. I'll go see if they have it at the front."

"Let me go." Ben stood up. "I need to return a few calls anyway. I'll be back soon." He smiled down at her, and his hand brushed her shoulder as he walked past and out the door.

"You're doing it again."

Jade turned to her daughter. "Doing what? What are you talking about?" she asked, even though she had a feeling she already knew the answer.

"You were staring at him again."

"No, I wasn't."

"Yes, you were. And you looked just like this." Dez puckered up her lips into a kissing face. Jade couldn't keep from laughing.

"You better be careful, or he'll come in here and see you doing that."

"Come in here and see you doing what?" Ben's voice at the door made Jade jump. He flashed a grin. "Sorry. I left my phone. Did I miss anything important?"

"Just the part where Mommy said she wanted to kiss you."

Jade felt the heat rush to her face. "No, I most certainly did not say that."

"Yes, you did." Dez smacked her lips together noisily.

"That's enough." Jade could hardly force herself to meet Ben's eyes to see his response.

He kept his focus on Dez. "Well, tell your mom that kissing is something very special. You should only do it with someone you care about very much." He grinned. "See you in a few minutes."

After he left, Jade leaned closer to her daughter. "What do you think you're doing, talking like that?" She didn't know if she was more angry or mortified.

Dez shrugged. "I was only trying to help."

Jade searched her daughter's face for the tell-tale signs of sassiness, but they were missing. "Well, don't do it again. You'll make me die of embarrassment."

"I didn't know adults got embarrassed."

"Well, they do. Especially when you're talking about your mother kissing someone she hardly knows."

"You know him well enough. And you do want to kiss him, don't you, Mama?"

"Just lie down and get some rest. Aren't you supposed to be sick or something?"

Dez grinned. "I still think that you should ask Ben on a date."

Jade pointed her finger in her daughter's face. "There you go again. What have I told you about talking like that?"

Dez sighed loudly. "Sorry. I mean you should ask *Officer* Ben on a date."

CHAPTER 40

Lab reports came in that afternoon. The drug in Dez's IV could have been fatal, but she'd received antidotes soon enough that nobody expected serious complications.

"I wouldn't be too surprised if she was a little drowsier than normal," the doctor explained.

"I should be so lucky." Jade grinned at her daughter.

"Hey." Dez gave a playful pout.

Right before dinnertime, the nurse came in with all the discharge paperwork and instructions. The timing couldn't have been more perfect, since Pastor Reggie and his family were due to land at the airport any minute. Thankfully the pastor's van would have enough space to fit Jade, Dez, and Ben. It would be midnight or maybe even later by the time they reached Glennallen, but at least they could spend the night at their home.

Two different police officers stopped by to hear Jade's story about shooting Gabriel at the cabin. Ben assured her it was standard procedure and that she didn't have anything to worry about. She wanted to trust him, but she still had a hard time believing the justice system would be completely fair and unbiased toward her. Hopefully, the fact that Gabriel had held Jade at gunpoint, that the gun she'd shot him with was his own, and that he was one of the men who'd abducted her daughter would free her of any murder charges. Ben knew a lawyer in Anchorage he promised to get her in touch with, even suggesting he might help her out *pro bono* if she ended up needing legal advice.

Jade was thankful for his help. Thankful that in this sea of cops in their imposing uniforms, she had someone she could count on as a friend. An ally. Ben spent nearly the entire day at the hospital, laughing when a therapy dog came in to cheer Dez up with some tricks, keeping Jade supplied with as much coffee as she could ever want.

"You sure you're not getting too bored with plain old black?" he asked, his teasing eyes twinkling.

She grinned back. "Are you saying a little cream might do me some good?"

"Never know unless you try."

It was nice to have a friend.

After all the discharge paperwork was filled out, Dez hopped into a wheelchair to head downstairs. While she kicked her light-up tennis shoes on the foot rests, Ben insisted on taking a few selfies with her. "It's not every kid who gets to ride their own chariot. I don't think even Elsa had one of these in *Frozen,* did she?"

"Elsa could have made one out of ice."

Ben smiled. "But I bet she wouldn't have looked as smart as you do, though."

Halfway down the hallway, he asked the nurse if he could be the one behind the wheelchair. "Now I can say I've pushed a real princess around."

Jade worried he was spoiling her daughter. Most days, it took all of Jade's energy to get them to the daycare on time and come home and crash on the couch for a few minutes before it was time to heat up something for dinner. She was thankful for all of Ben's attention, but she hoped Dez wouldn't be disappointed when they got back to Glennallen and life returned to normal.

At least the daycare was closed for Christmas break. Jade would try to find the energy to do some arts and crafts with Dez. Maybe bake some cookies. The downside was that no work meant such a meager paycheck at the end of the month. She still wasn't sure what she was going to do about presents. How sad was it that just a few hours after promising God to be better mom if he only brought her daughter back to her, Jade was reverting right back to her old tired, worried self, stressed out about money, easily annoyed if Dez asked too many questions or demanded too much out of her.

Ben wheeled Dez into the hospital gift shop, insisting that she pick out anything she wanted. Jade watched them, despising the familiar feeling of guilt that seemed to permeate her entire life as a mother. Guilt she wasn't doing enough, buying enough, being enough for her daughter. Ben was nice, but Jade couldn't shake the feeling that he was showing off.

See? Being a parent is easy. Look how good at it I already am, and she's not even mine.

Ben would never know what it felt like to be Dez's mom. To be so terrified for her daughter's safety you nearly threw up. To experience those heart palpitations and that cold sweat every time you thought about what might have happened. What had already happened.

Kids are resilient. It was something Jade had been telling herself for years, ever since Dez was a baby and managed to roll herself off the bed and land on the hard, wooden floor.

"Kids are resilient," the phone nurse said, calming Jade's fears, assuaging her guilt.

Maybe the nurse was right. Jade watched her daughter

in the gift store checkout line, holding two new books plus a giant Elsa balloon she'd conned Ben into buying for her. There was no visible indication that her daughter had just survived a kidnapping, a night in the woods, and a poisoning attempt. Dez was smiling, playful, and as lively as always.

Kids are resilient. Maybe Dez had already bounced back from all the fear and trauma she'd endured. But what if she was carrying it beneath the surface? What if the trauma wouldn't come out for months or even years? Would Jade wake up when her daughter was a high-schooler only to learn that Dez's eating disorders and propensity to self-harm all stemmed back from the past twenty-four hours?

Someone like Ben didn't have to worry about that. All he had to do was crack jokes and hand over his credit card to the cashier behind the counter. Jade had no idea how much money Alaska state troopers made, but it was certainly more than a thirty-hour-a-week daycare employee.

"You're doing it again, Mom," were the first words out of Dez's mouth when Ben wheeled her out of the store. Jade wasn't about to argue and risk Ben's overhearing. She pried her eyes away from him and smiled at her daughter.

"Ready to go home, baby?"

Dez nodded. "Yeah. But can we make a quick stop first? Officer Ben's gonna buy me a big old hamburger with lots of French fries. And ice cream, too."

CHAPTER 41

Jade had never been happier to find herself on the Glenn Highway, headed for home.

Dez knew Pastor Reggie's kids from Sunday school, and she was happy to sit in the back of the van with them. With Reggie and his wife up front, that left enough space for Jade and Ben to sit side by side on the long drive back to Glennallen.

Reggie had a cough and was losing his voice. His wife was exhausted after a week in the Lower 48 with two little kids and was asleep about ten minutes into the drive.

Jade took advantage of the relative silence to think. At some point, it would probably hit her that she'd killed a man. She should also be more concerned that Sapphire was still alive. But right now, she was fixating on Christmas, wondering how she could move things around to find money for Dez's gifts. The heating bill wouldn't be due until after the New Year, but with such a small paycheck coming in at the end of the month, she couldn't afford to waste a penny. She had no idea if the oil company would actually turn off heat to a home with a single mom and five-year-old girl, but she didn't feel like testing her luck.

"Sounds like they're having fun," Ben observed after a round of giggles erupted from the back seat.

"Yeah, they're pretty good friends."

"I'm glad you two are on your way home."

"So am I." She glanced over at him. There were so many things it felt like they should be talking about. Like the fact that Jade would have to answer for her role in Gabriel's death. That she'd seen people of color denied justice too many times, and she was scared.

That the woman who tried to abduct her daughter was still alive.

One thing among many that Jade still didn't understand was the drugs in the IV. So far, Ben didn't have any updates about what the police had learned from the nurse they caught. Had Sapphire put him up to it? Why would she kidnap Dez only to try to kill her the next day?

Sapphire was nothing like the villains Jade had learned to fear. She was capricious, led by dreams and whims and *words of God* that could come from anywhere. It made her unpredictable.

And terrifying.

Ben let out a sigh. "Long day, huh?"

Jade only had the energy left to nod.

"Why don't you try to get some sleep?" he suggested, then cracked a grin. "I promise not to tease you if you snore."

CHAPTER 42

It was after midnight when Reggie pulled up in front of Jade's house. Ben insisted on double and triple checking every room, nook, and cranny before Jade locked herself in for the night. Some of her friends in Glennallen kept their doors unlocked, but even with its relatively low crime rate compared to places like Anchorage, Jade had always been careful and protective of her home, her belongings, and most of all her daughter.

Ben wasn't working tonight, but he said another trooper he knew would park outside her house and keep watch.

Dez had fallen asleep in the back of the van, and Jade was relieved that tonight she could tuck her daughter into her own bed. She just wished she could find that kind of rest herself. Even with a squad car in her driveway, Jade jumped at every noise, convinced that Sapphire had returned to finish what she'd started. Jade wouldn't admit it, but she was thankful when Ben called to check up on her. At one point, she even thought of erecting a barricade against the front door. When she wasn't freaking out over every single stray sound, she was terrified that Dez was sick, that her core temperature had dropped, or that the medicine dumped into her IV had caused her heart to fail.

Between investigating every noise and running into Dez's room to make sure she was still alive, Jade didn't get any more than three or four hours of sleep total. Eventually she gave up on her own bed, and she crawled on the mattress beside her daughter, snuggling her tight while she stared at Dez and worried. Worried that Sapphire was going to try to kidnap her again. Maybe even kill her. Worried that the events of the past two days would scar her, change her, transform the bright, fun, sassy little girl into a timid, frightened creature.

Worried that she still didn't have Christmas presents or money to buy any.

Years earlier, Jade had memorized verses about casting her cares on the Lord, trusting him to provide for all her needs, relying on him, and no longer living as a slave to fear. But as the endless midnight wore on, as her body kept reacting in terror to every single sound, every perceived change in her daughter's breathing, nothing she remembered helped.

A picture of Ben floated through her mind, an image of

him smiling and joking with her daughter. For a moment she experienced the peace and happiness she'd felt earlier when she was with him. Then the feelings vanished, and she was alone again in a dark, eerie room, with only her fears and her trauma there to comfort her.

CHAPTER 43

"Mama! Mama! Wake up!"

Jade opened her eyes. It was already light out. How long had she slept in?

"Mama! Look. Santa's here."

"It's not Christmas yet. Go to sleep, baby."

"No, Santa really is here. He just knocked on the door."

"What are you talking about?"

"Go see for yourself."

Jade glanced at the time. She threw on her slippers, tossed a dirty sweatshirt over her flannel pajamas, and peeked out the window.

Dez crossed her arms and jutted out her hip. "See? Told you it was Santa."

"That's not Santa, baby. I don't know who it is." Jade stared at the dressed-up man on her porch, wondering if she should call the troopers. The squad car that had been parked outside all night was gone. The man on the porch turned and caught her staring at him from the window.

Smiling, he waved as he set down a huge black trash bag.

"Look, Mama!" Dez exclaimed. "He's brung presents."

Jade hurried to the door, wishing she'd actually gotten dressed. "Ben, what are you doing here?"

"Ho, ho, ho," he declared, stepping into their home and lowering his very fake looking white beard. "I'm bringing you your gifts."

Jade stared at the bag he dumped on the floor. "What's this?"

"Presents for you and your little girl. Ho, ho, ho."

"You can talk normally, Ben." Dez ran to the trash bag. "We all know it's really you."

"That's *Officer* Ben," Jade corrected.

He took off his bright red hat and smiled.

She glared at her daughter. "Don't go opening that bag without permission," she told Dez. "Who taught you your manners, young lady? A moose?"

Dez giggled and pulled out a wrapped gift. "Look! I bet this is one of those huge coloring books." She pulled a package out and shook it. "And these must be the colored pencils. I hope there's a pencil sharpener in here too because mine's broke."

"Dezzirea Rose Jackson," Jade huffed.

"It's okay with me if she opens them now," Ben said

quietly. "These are from everyone around town. People brought them to the church yesterday. The sled and new mittens and snow boots are from the trooper's station. So are the ice skates."

Dez's eyes widened. "Ice skates?" She turned the whole bag upside down, spilling at least two dozen packages onto the floor.

"That package with the blue snowflake paper is for your mom," Ben said, "so don't open it." He glanced at Jade. "I heard that someone around here might need a new coffee maker." He pulled a plastic grocery bag out of the mix. "And I brought you creamer. I hear it's an acquired taste."

Jade didn't meet his eyes. "You really shouldn't have gone to all this trouble." Jade stared at the booty, wondering how much of it would be broken or lost by January first.

Ben scratched beneath his Santa beard then finally took it off. "The only trouble was getting into this suit. I had no idea it'd be so itchy. We rented it for the troopers Christmas party tonight. Which is actually one more reason why I wanted to stop by." He dusted a piece of white cotton fuzz off his suit's belly, lowering his gaze. "I know it's short notice, but I was wondering if you'd be my plus one."

"Tonight?"

He nodded. "We're having prime rib. And I hear the captain's wife makes a mean pumpkin pie."

Jade glanced at her daughter, who fortunately seemed more interested in unwrapping her gifts than in eavesdropping.

"I've got to take Dez to church for her Christmas rehearsal tonight. Otherwise it sounds like a great time." She licked her lips, hoping he wouldn't be too upset.

He moved his Santa hat from one hand to the other. "What if I told you that Aisha already agreed to take Dez home after rehearsal?"

"You talked to Aisha?"

He smiled. "Guilty."

She stared at the buckle of his Santa suit. "I don't know. With all she's gone through …"

Dez glanced up. "Come on, Mama. You should go to the party with Officer Ben. You'll have a great time."

"I don't want to leave you alone, baby. Besides, this is a grown-up conversation, and I don't remember asking your opinion."

"Yeah, but he's invited you, and it would be mean to say no."

Ben grinned. "That smart girl of yours has got a point

there."

He really wasn't making it easy for her to turn him down. And when he gave her one last, hopeful smile, Jade realized she didn't want to.

"Okay. What time do I need to be ready?"

CHAPTER 44

"No, Mama. It's a Christmas party, so you have to wear red."

"But I think this black dress makes me look skinnier."

Dez scrunched up her face. "Why would you want to look skinnier?"

"It's just what people do when they get to be old like … oh, never mind. So you really think the red one's nicer?" She held up the dress on the hanger.

Dez nodded. "Uh-huh. It's more like a party. The black one would just make you look like …" She cocked her head to the side and considered. "Like a lump of coal."

"Well, thank you very much, Miss Fashionista."

She shrugged. "It's what I'm here for."

"Well, you go scram now so I can get dressed. And you better have all those new toys off the floor by the time I come out or I'm taking them away for two whole weeks. Got that?"

"Okay." Dez jumped off the bed and scrambled down

the hall. Jade shut the door and eyed both dresses one more time. She didn't want to wear the red one. She hadn't even asked Ben how fancy tonight was supposed to be. The black dress was simple and elegant. If she wore the red, everyone would think she was trying to stand out. Like Rudolph's nose or a giant pimple.

Well, maybe after all she'd gone through there was nothing wrong with standing out. At least not a little. And she did have a pair of heels that would go great with it.

Jade squeezed into the red dress, the one she'd bought herself two years ago as an incentive to lose weight. She'd never lost the pounds, but she managed to zip it up with a little help from her daughter. Jade had just finished applying her makeup when someone knocked on the door.

"I'll get it!" Dez called from the other room. Jade sprinted to intercept her. For all the danger she'd been in, Dez didn't seem to have a single scared bone in her body. Her carefree recklessness made Jade nervous.

She glanced out the window, saw Ben in his trooper uniform looking crisp and clean, and opened the door. "Hello."

He stepped in, and a blush settled on his pale cheeks. For a minute, it looked like he didn't know if he was supposed to give her a hug, kiss her cheek, or stretch out his hand for a hearty shake.

Jade took a step back, hoping to save him his dignity.

"You look nice," he finally said.

"You're supposed to tell her she looks *beautiful*," Dez announced.

Jade gave her daughter a warning look.

"You ladies ready?" Ben asked, holding the door open.

"Yup," Jade answered. "Just let me close up, and we'll be right out."

Jade checked the lock twice, glanced at herself one last time in the small mirror, and followed Ben out the door toward his car.

CHAPTER 45

It was stupid for Jade to leave home with nothing but her shawl to keep her warm. Even in the community hall, she shivered each time someone new came in, bringing icy gusts of freezing air with them.

When she agreed to attend Ben's Christmas party with him, she'd failed to consider that most of the people he worked with had been actively involved in her daughter's search. Between congratulations, well-wishes, and questions about Dez, Jade hardly got a chance to talk with Ben before dinner was served.

The meal was delicious, a no-expense-spared ordeal that Ben and the others dug into with gusto. Jade took small bites, wishing she had stayed home tonight. Even when she walked Dez into the church to drop her off at her Christmas play rehearsal, Jade tried changing plans, tempting her daughter with promises of ice cream and hot chocolate both.

Dez would hear nothing of it.

Jade didn't feel right being separated. After all both of them had gone through, they needed each other.

At least Jade needed her daughter.

"You okay?" Ben asked as couples started to get up from the table to enjoy some music. "I was going to ask if you'd like to dance, but I'm a little scared of those heels you're wearing."

Jade tried to match his smile. It wasn't his fault that tonight had been a bust. He'd certainly tried to make everything perfect, from the small bottle of somewhat generic perfume he gave her in the car to arranging for Aisha to babysit after Dez's play practice was done.

"Did you eat too much dinner?" Ben asked. "I know I did."

Jade sighed. She'd gotten herself all made up, hoping to make a good impression on Ben and his coworkers. All that to realize she couldn't pretend to be anything other than what she was. And right now, she was a worried mom who was anxious about her daughter.

And her feet were killing her.

"I'm sorry." She searched Ben's eyes. Did he understand? "Everything's been great, and dinner was really nice, but I can't stop worrying about Dez. I really shouldn't have agreed to leave her tonight. It's too soon."

She watched his expression for signs of disappointment. He smiled gently then nodded. "That makes sense. I'm sorry."

She reached out and touched the sleeve of his shirt. It was a small gesture but felt somehow intimate. "Don't be. I'm glad you invited me. And maybe if things hadn't just happened like they did ..."

"I understand. Should we call it a night?"

"If you want to stay here, I can call Aisha. I'm sure she wouldn't mind picking me up."

"Don't be silly. We'll go pick up Dez, and then I'll take you both back to your place."

"Thank you, Ben." She held his gaze for a quiet moment.

His sad, almost tired expression softened into a smile. "Don't mention it. That's what friends are for."

CHAPTER 46

"So, where are we going?" Ben asked as they rolled out of the parking lot. Behind them, Jade could still hear the sound of the Christmas music blaring out the community hall windows.

"I don't know if Dez is still at the church or not. Let me give Aisha a text."

She opened her purse. "Uh-oh."

"What's the matter?"

"I left my phone at home."

"Well, there's the church up ahead. I don't see any lights on. Do you?"

"No, they must be finished. Do you mind swinging by Aisha's house?"

"Of course not."

"It's about two miles up the Glenn. You turn at the first stop after the clinic."

"I can do that."

Jade tried to think of something else to say. She'd

already apologized for ending the night so early, but even though he'd been gracious about it, she still didn't think she'd told Ben everything.

Like how she hoped he'd give her another chance soon.

Was this going to be life from now on? Was she always going to be this nervous, unable to spend ten or twenty minutes away from her daughter without breaking into a cold sweat and heart palpitations?

How did you just pick up after something like this and make life go back to normal?

Ben turned onto Aisha's road, and Jade directed him toward her friend's driveway. He pulled in, and Jade unbuckled her seatbelt. "I'll be back in just a minute."

"I'll be here waiting."

Something in his tone caught her off guard. She turned to look, fully expecting to see something different, but there was that same kind and open expression. The gentle smile he probably gave to everyone.

"Be right back," she repeated and shut the car door behind her.

If it hadn't been for her ridiculous heels and the fear that Ben might be watching her, she would have run. Even though she'd tried to stay composed, she'd been trembling on the ride over here, and now that she was so close to her daughter, she wanted nothing but to find Dez and crush her in a strong bear hug.

She knocked on Aisha's door and stood shivering in the cold.

"Jade?"

"Yeah, I'm sorry I didn't text. I left my phone at home. We decided to call it an early night. How's Dez been?"

Jade had been so relieved at the thought of having her daughter back with her, it took a few seconds to recognize the confused expression on Aisha's face. When it sunk in, her racing pulse stopped, crashed to a halt. "What's wrong?"

Aisha shook her head. "Nothing. Did Ben drive you over?"

"Yeah. Why?"

Aisha twisted the bracelet she was wearing and kept her voice low. "I wanted to talk to you about something while you're here. I can drive you home in a little bit if that's okay with you."

Jade studied her friend. "Sure. Did Dez get into trouble?"

Aisha winced. "No, nothing like that. Could you just let Ben know I'll take you home in a bit?"

"Sure." Jade paused before turning around, trying to

guess what Aisha wanted to say.

Ben rolled down his window as she approached his side of the car.

"I'm going to hang out here for a while and grab a ride home later with Aisha," she told him.

"Everything okay?"

She nodded, trying to believe it was true. "Yeah. We just haven't had a chance to talk through everything yet. She's a pretty good friend. Just wanted to have a little girl time." At least that's what Jade hoped was going on.

Ben nodded. "All right. Tell Dez good night for me."

"I will. And thanks for everything. The dinner, the party, the perfume. I …" She stopped herself. She couldn't really say *I had a great time*. He'd know that wasn't true. "I hope we get to do something like this again soon."

Ben smiled. "Me, too."

She figured he'd say something like that just to be polite. Tonight might have been the worst date he'd ever been on, but at least he wasn't making this any harder on her. She paused in the driveway, wondering if there was anything more to say. "Well, goodnight," she finally offered.

"Goodnight."

She walked slowly back up to Aisha's front door,

listening to the sound of his tires rolling back down the driveway. Jade stepped up to the porch and let herself in. The first thing she saw was her friend lying on the floor.

The next thing she saw was Sapphire holding a knife up to her daughter's throat.

CHAPTER 47

"Don't move a muscle." Sapphire was shorter than Jade, but she kept her eyes level with hers.

"What are you doing?" Jade didn't move forward but studied her daughter from head to toe to see if she'd been hurt.

"Just obeying God's word." A smile spread across Sapphire's face. "Why don't you come in. Nice place your friend has here, isn't it?"

Jade looked down at Aisha. "What'd you do to her?"

"She'll be fine. I just needed her to get that trooper to go home, and now she's served her purpose. Come on. I hate standing in doorways. Feels so rude."

Sapphire backed up slowly until she was in Aisha's living room. "Take a seat."

Jade shook her head. "I'll stand, thanks."

Sapphire paused for a moment before shrugging. "Suit yourself."

More than anything, Jade wanted to talk to her

daughter. To tell Dez that everything would be okay. She tried to read her daughter's expression. What was going on?

Sapphire sat down in Aisha's white plush reclining chair, positioning Dez on her lap, careful to keep the knife just a centimeter from her throat. Jade balled her hands into fists. Her senses drowned out everything but Sapphire, her cruel and striking face, the melodic cadence of her speech.

"My husband often preached that discipleship is costly. If we want to experience the full riches of God's destiny in our lives, we must be prepared to make sacrifices. He still tests his children today, just like he did when he told Abraham to take his son up on Mount Moriah and sacrifice him as a burnt offering."

Jade kept her eyes on Sapphire but took in her surroundings, hunting for anything that might serve as a weapon. A metal bar, a vase, anything she could throw. But what could she do without risking her daughter's life?

She searched Dez's face, but her daughter's expression was unreadable.

Jade's soul recoiled when Sapphire resumed her speech.

"Last night, God told me that he was going to heal my shoulder where you shot me. He also told me that he was going to test my faith. I didn't know what he meant until I heard that your daughter was in the hospital, and I knew what I had to do. Isaac was the child of promise, but God still commanded Abraham to carry him up to that mountain, to tie him on that altar and sacrifice him there.

"I didn't want to do it." If Sapphire had been any other human being talking about anything other than Dez's attempted murder, Jade would have thought those were actual tears born from true emotion. "I told God I love this little girl as if she were my own. She's my child of promise." She held Dez closer. Jade didn't know which worried her more, the knife so close to her daughter's throat, or Dez's expressionless face. Jade wasn't even certain if her daughter knew she was there in the room with her.

Was this some kind of psychological protective mechanism? Was God allowing Dez's brain to shut down momentarily so she wouldn't experience the fear and the horror of what she was going through? Or had Sapphire already done something to her?

Jade's stomach churned to see the way Sapphire wrapped her free arm around her daughter's body. "Thankfully, like Abraham, God saw that I was faithful. He saw that I'd rather see this child of promise dead than disobey his word. I set out to do what he told me last night it was my duty to fulfill, and now he's blessed me with this sweet child to call my own."

"She'll never be yours," Jade hissed.

Sapphire waved her hand as if she were swatting away a fly. "God's already shown me our future together. Mother and daughter leading others to their glorious destinies in Christ." She leaned in and kissed Dez on the cheek.

It was too much to endure. "Dez," Jade snapped. "Dezzirae Rose Jackson."

Sapphire shook her head. "I've prayed over her. Prayed that God would protect her from the lies you'd try to use to woo her back to you. Her destiny and her future are already sealed. The only thing you have to worry about now is making this transition as easy for her as possible."

"You're insane."

Sapphire smirked. "Christ's followers have been called worse things throughout history. As for me, I count it a joy and an honor to suffer slander for the sake of my Savior and King."

Jade would do anything to make Sapphire shut up. She'd already shot her once. She'd do it again if she had the right weapon, only this time she'd be sure to check the body afterwards to make sure she did as thorough a job as possible.

"I know you're angry and confused," Sapphire went on, "but this doesn't have to hurt at all. In fact, I'd like to pray for you, to ask God to make your passing as peaceful as a baby falling to sleep at its mother's breast."

Jade knew there was only one way out of her situation. She started to laugh.

"What's so funny?" Sapphire demanded.

"You are." Jade tried to hold it in, but soon her sides ached from the chuckles that shook her whole body. "You're nothing but an old, pathetic, dried up nobody who thinks you're important because your husband called himself a pastor. You're both nobodies. In fact, you're worse than nobodies. You think you're righteous and holy and doing God's work, but I wouldn't trade spots with you on the day of judgment in a million years."

Sapphire pointed the knife blade toward Jade. "What does the Bible say about speaking badly against the leaders of your people?"

"You're not my leader. You're nothing to me. Your husband was a dirty, manipulative old man who died lonely and pathetic. The only future he deserved to see was the inside of a jail cell, and that's where you're going to rot away like the miserable piece of trash you are."

The plan was working. Pushing Dez aside, Sapphire

rose from the seat, lurching toward her.

Jade was ready. She lifted her knee, ramming it into Sapphire's gut. The knife clattered to the floor. Sapphire reached down, but Jade got to it first. While Sapphire pummeled her from above, Jade grabbed the handle with one hand and Sapphire's long hair with the other. Wincing in disgust, Jade stabbed once. Twice. A third time until she was certain Sapphire had given up her attack.

Then she ran to her daughter.

CHAPTER 48

"Baby? Baby? Can you hear me? It's Mama."

Jade knelt beside her daughter, her fingers shaking while she tried to dial 911 on Aisha's cell phone. She waved her hand and snapped her fingers in front of her daughter's face while she waited for the call to go through.

"Baby, look at me. It's over now. We're going to be okay."

Ben was the first to arrive on the scene. The ambulance crew was only a minute behind.

"Is she dead?" Jade asked as Ben leaned over Sapphire's body.

"No."

A clash of emotions raced through Jade's body. Relief. Disappointment. Confusion.

Ben walked over to Dez. "Can you hear me, sweetheart? Are you hurt at all?"

"She's been like that since I got here," Jade explained, holding her daughter tight.

"Probably the shock. But we should take her to the clinic to make sure."

"What about Aisha?"

"Hit to the head," he explained. "She'll have a nasty headache, maybe a concussion, but the paramedics don't think it's anything to get too worried about."

Jade took her daughter's hand. "Baby, you want to come with me to talk to the nurse at the clinic? Make sure you're doing okay?" There was nothing in the world Jade wouldn't give up in order to hear some kind of sassy reply. Tears leaked down Jade's cheeks. "I don't know what's wrong with her."

"She's all right," Ben answered. "Probably just scared." He reached out his hand and rested it on Dez's shoulder. "You know what, princess? All the bad guys who wanted to hurt you are gone now. You don't have anything to be afraid of anymore."

Jade waited for some sign of life to light up her daughter's expression.

Nothing.

She squeezed her eyes shut. She couldn't stand to see her daughter like this.

"Hey, Dez?" Ben asked. "Want to go for a ride to the clinic with me? Want to take a trip with your good pal

Ben?"

Dez blinked, and a small, quivering smile spread across her lips. "I think you mean *Officer* Ben, don't you?"

CHAPTER 49

Christmas Eve

Ben knelt down and adjusted the halo of Dez's angel costume. "That was the best Bible verse reading I've ever heard, young lady."

She beamed at him. "I memorized it myself."

"Yeah, well, I bet your mom helped a lot, too."

She shook her head. "Nope. Only a little." She slipped her hand into Ben's. "Come on. Didn't you hear Pastor Reggie say there's cake downstairs?"

Ben hesitated for just a moment, glancing at Jade. "You coming?"

Jade adjusted her earrings and nodded at him. He slipped his hand behind her back then leaned in. "Mmm. What's that beautiful smell?"

"That's Mama's perfume you gave her," Dez announced. "She wears it all the time because she says it reminds her of you and how you kissed her that night the

217

crazy lady got arrested."

Ben raised his eyebrows. "I thought you were asleep in the backseat when that happened."

Dez shook her head proudly. "Nope. I'm just a really good actor."

He chuckled. "Yes, you are. Your performance tonight was bar none."

Dez pouted. "What's that mean?"

"It means you were fabulous, baby," Jade answered. "Now leave Mr. Ben alone."

"Don't you mean *Officer* Ben?"

They made their way downstairs, and Dez rushed toward the dessert table.

Ben turned and faced Jade, taking both her hands in his. "So she's doing well?"

Jade nodded. "Yeah. She's talking with a social worker at the clinic about what happened, and we'll drive in to see a play therapist in Palmer next week. From everything I can tell, she's doing fine. I'm the one who still feels like a wreck around here."

He leaned in and rested his forehead against hers. "I think you're doing a wonderful job."

Jade squeezed his hands. "So, you're still coming over for Christmas dinner at Aisha's tomorrow, right?"

"Yeah, what time should I be there?"

"Around three, but don't expect to eat until five or later."

"How's Aisha after getting knocked out, by the way? I haven't talked to her since that night in the clinic."

"She's fine. They ended up sending her to Valdez for an MRI just to be safe, but the swelling was already way down, and she's back to her normal self."

"That's good."

Upstairs, a Christmas carol soundtrack played loudly enough to be heard over the laughter and conversations in the fellowship hall. Jade looked around at her friends from Glennallen Bible Church, men and women had braved the cold to search for her daughter, families who had donated some of their own presents to make sure Dez had plenty of new toys, far more than she would ever need.

It was a hodgepodge collection of young and old and far from a perfect assembly. Pastor Reggie was still suffering from laryngitis and could barely croak out tonight's closing prayer. His small son had fallen asleep backstage, leaving the bottom half of the donkey to complete his role without a head. While folks mingled around the dessert table, a mother scolded her teenage daughter, and a husband who was known to only come to church when his wife dragged him in on holidays was sulking in the corner.

If you were to poll everyone here, each one would probably have a handful of suggestions on how to make Glennallen Bible a better church. Some were vocal in their complaints about the music, the children's ministry, or the way the pastor's kids fidgeted in their seats. But tonight, there was no other group of people Jade wanted to spend the holidays with.

Tonight, she truly felt at home.

A NOTE FROM THE AUTHOR

I hope you enjoyed *Frost Heaves*, which is my third suspense novel set in Glennallen. I feel so blessed to call Alaska home, and I'm so happy to be able to share snippets of life in the great, frosty north.

If you enjoyed *Frost Heaves*, and if you're ready for more Christian suspense with strong-willed characters who learn to rely on God in the scariest of circumstances, you'll love *Blessing on the Run*, another wintery novel about a single mom trying to protect her child.

Blessing will do anything to keep her son safe.

Even return to the horrific life she was delivered from so many years earlier.

For another spine-tingling suspense, grab your copy of *Blessing on the Run* today. (Just be prepared to stay up late!)

Printed in Great Britain
by Amazon

62339931R00135